HIS LOVE WAS LAW

K. RENEE

D1502831

Chapter One

LOVE

Thank god I only had two-morning classes today. I had just walked in my room and my roommate, Erica, was placing her books in her bag.

"Hey Love, I'm going to class. I will see you later tonight," Erica stated.

"Okay, boo, see you later!" I shouted out as I went to change into my tank top and shorts. I was taking my ass back to bed.

"Oh damn, are you looking for me?" I heard Erica say.

"Nah, is Love here?" the familiar voice asked, and I walked out to see who the hell was asking for me. It was my best friend Law and I was excited to see him standing there. It has been a minute; I have truly missed him.

"What are you doing up here?" I asked Law, as he stepped in my dorm room.

"I came to see your nappy headed ass. Do I need an excuse to be here?" he looked at me as he plopped down on my bed.

"I guess not, are you coming back for my graduation?" I questioned, sitting down beside him and grabbed my bag of chips that he had so kindly helped himself to.

"Love, that is a crazy ass question, we have been best friends since the sandbox. Why the hell wouldn't I be at your graduation?" he looked over at me.

"I was just checking," I replied, as he snatched my damn chips back.

"Put some clothes on, Sin is downstairs, we're going to the mall. I want you to get everything you need for your graduation day," he spoke as he texted on his phone.

"Who are you texting, one of your plethora of women?" I questioned.

"Mind the business that pays you, and go get dressed," he glanced at me, and directed his attention right back on his phone.

I was attending school at the University of Delaware and I couldn't believe that Law and Sin drove down here from Philly just to see me. They do come to visit me but it's always on the weekend, never on a weekday, and the visits are rare. I have always wanted to be a pharmacist and my dream was coming true; I was almost at the finish line. Even though I was graduating in a few days, I still had another four years of schooling to go. This is the life I chose, and I'm here for it all.

It took me thirty minutes, but I was finally dressed, and ready to go spend his money.

"Okay, I'm ready," I looked over at him, he was just staring at me.

"What?" I asked him, as I looked down at myself. I thought something was wrong with what I had on.

"Nothing, let's go," he said grabbing my hand and pulling me out the door. On our way to his car, I ran into my new boo Zion. We have been dating for about eight months, it was nothing serious. He's been pressuring me about being in an exclusive relationship with him. I just couldn't commit right now; I was trying to stay focused on my education.

"Love, what's up, where are you headed?" he questioned looking over at Law.

"Hey Zi, this is my best friend Law that I was telling you about. Law this is my friend Zion," I introduced.

"What's up? L, come on before Sin gets in his bag," Law spoke, pulling me away.

"Zi, I will call you when I get back," I told him, as Law damn near dragged me to the car.

"Why are we moving so damn fast?" I asked when we made it to the car.

"Who was that nigga? He is obviously trying to be more than just a friend, by the way he was looking at your ass," Law said as he opened the door so that I could get in the car.

"That's my little boo thang, he's on the Basketball team and we've been kicking it for a while now. He is entering the

NBA draft soon. He's really good, you should check him out," I told Law.

"Nah, I'm good," he said and got in the driver's seat. I didn't know what was up with him and his sudden mood change, so I just brushed it off.

"Sin, what's up?" I asked sitting up.

"What it do, L Boogie?" he responded turning to give me that million-dollar smile.

I must admit Law and Sin were fine, and I mean that shit with every bit of my womanhood. We all grew up in the same hood around Twenty-First and Diamond. Though they had different fathers and the same mom, both shared a golden-brown complexion. Law and Sin kept their hair neatly trimmed in low-cut fades and were fine in their own right, with muscular builds and tattoo adorned bodies. Law was bigger, and his body was more defined, but women were always trying to get next to both of them. There was always somebody in their damn face, and they loved that shit.

Sin was a few years older than us. Law and I were the closest, we did everything together unless he decided to hang with one of his hoochies. Law and Sin were street dudes and worked under Law's Dad Jax. Mr. Jax was fine as hell; I see where my bestie got his looks from because daddy was giving these chicks the business.

I was twenty-two years old and an only child. Drugs are my mother Evelyn's best friend, and I never knew my dad. I think I got my shape from my mother; my wide hips and big ass always attracted the attention of every man I came across.

The shit was damn near irritating at times, my looks must have come from my father. I'm sure I had his eye color, because no one in my family had light brown eyes. My mom was a beautiful woman, but the drugs just took over her life and she let herself go.

I tried so many times to get my mom off the drugs. I cried many nights wondering what I did wrong for her to choose drugs over me. Thank God for my Grandmother, Law, and my cousin Tay. Through it all they were the ones that were there for me, my cousin Tay was my best friend, she went to school in New York and graduated two years ago. She decided that she wanted to stay there and work in her field. Because of that we don't see each other as much as we would have liked. My grandmother raised me, and she did the best she could with what she had. I never wanted for anything and she made sure of that. All she ever asked of me is to make sure I got my education. I graduated at the top of my class in high school, and I was graduating college with a 4.0 GPA.

I tried so hard to get Law to go to college, he was a genius when it came to drawing. He always talked about getting enough money saved up to open his own tattoo shop. It has been years and he hasn't done that shit yet. I sent up a prayer daily for my friend, hoping that one day he would see that it was so much more to life than a street corner.

"Damn, Taj is going to drive my ass crazy," Sin spoke as his girl Taj called his phone for the twentieth time.

"I don't know why you keep messing with her ass. I

thought you said you broke it off with her?" Law shook his head.

"I did, and that's why her ass keeps calling. I'm trying to see what's up with this chick Diamond, but Taj ass just won't let me be great," Sin let out an exasperated sigh.

"I told y'all to stop making these girls think you're going to be with them. Just be upfront and you won't have these problems," I told them, as we pulled into the mall parking lot.

"Girl, we not making them think shit, the dick making them go crazy. I can't help that I lay the pipe good, fuck that! If they can't handle the magic stick, then that's on them! I don't have time for a damn relationship, my focus is getting this money," Law spoke as we got out of the car.

"That's what the fuck I'm saying, they don't call me big dick Sin, for nothing!" Sin laughed, and I just shook my head at these two damn clowns.

"I swear y'all gone meet your match one day and I hope she breaks y'all asses down to your knees," I told them as we walked into Nordstrom's.

"She gotta be a bad muthafucka to do that shit, and if there is a woman alive that can break me down like that. I'm marrying her ass point blank period! She can get all I fucking got; I will turn in my black phone asap!" Sin responded.

"Black phone, what the fuck is that?" I laughed, because I know he had something crazy that was going to roll off his tongue.

"Back in the day, you would hear the OG's saying they got a black book. Well, I'm a muthafuckin new school nigga. I'm not walking around with no damn black book; I have a special phone for all my jumps. I call it the black phone; you better get you one." We all fell out laughing. This boy has lost his mind.

"Bruh, your ass ain't getting married, no matter how good the pussy is," Law stated.

"What about you Law, if you meet the right girl would you marry her?" I asked just to see where his head was at.

"I might, it all depends on where I am in my life. I have to have my shit together before I get married. I mean I got a lil' money, not enough to take care of no family. We just starting out, I know our time is coming soon. I'm trying to build some shit right now, once I have my future secured, I will start my family. But you know shit happens and sometimes it doesn't always go the way you plan it. I guess I will just have to deal with it when it comes my way," he looked at me and shrugged.

"I hear you best, now let's do some shopping," I told him, for some reason the way he looked at me had me looking at him a little different. We shopped for damn near four hours and were finally leaving the mall. I was set for graduation, Law and Sin made sure I had everything I needed and then some. By the time we got back to my dorm, it was a little after seven and Zi was standing out front talking to some of his friends.

"Damn that nigga must have smelt you from the highway," Law said, getting out the car to help me with my bags.

"Law, hush, Zi is a nice guy and I like him," I told him grabbing the bag out of his hand.

"I hear you, love bug. Let me help you take your things

upstairs," he replied, as we walked up to the doors where Zi was standing.

"Hey, you need some help?" Zi asked me.

"Nah, we good," Law spoke and held the door for me to walk in.

"I will be back in a few minutes, Zi," I smiled at him and walked in with Law behind me.

"Don't get too wrapped up with that dude, you need to focus on what's important and that's school," Law said to me placing my things on my bed.

"Law, I got this," I responded.

"Alright, I gotta get back to Philly. I will see you Saturday. Let me know if there is anything else you need. I love you, love bug," he said, kissing my cheek and pulling me in for a hug.

"Love you too, best," I whispered as the hug he was giving me lasted a little longer than usual. This entire visit with Law was weird as hell, I'm not sure what's going on with him. I guess he will tell me if there is something that I needed to know.

Chapter Two

LAW

I'm not sure when my feelings changed for Love, but that shit seems like it hit me overnight. I have to get my shit together; I don't want anything fucking up the friendship that we have. Besides, my mom would kill me if I took it there with Love. She said I wasn't ready for a girl, because I was too busy being a hoe. My mother didn't care what came out of her mouth. She loved Love and didn't want me to hurt her with my bullshit. I would never hurt Love; I would do anything to protect her and the relationship that we've built over the years. I've noticed that the more I'm around her, the more my feelings come out on display. If I can't get my feelings in check, I'm just gonna have to shoot my shot. This fucking Zion dude that she fuckin with almost caught it today.

"Yo Jax said he needs us to stop by his crib asap, I told him we would stop by as soon as we hit the city," Sin spoke when I got back in the car and pulled off.

"Did he say what he wanted?" I asked.

"Nah, you know that nigga ain't giving no details over the phone," Sin sat back in his seat and got comfortable, as we headed back to Philly to see what my pop wanted. The shit between me and my dad wasn't great, but we weren't on bad terms. I just didn't fuck with the nigga all the time. The way he did my mom was fucked up, but the nigga was still my dad and my mother was still fucking with his ass.

He didn't just leave me out here to take care of myself, he did help out until I was eighteen. Then his slime ball ass made me work for my money, by working for his ass. My brother and I did drop offs and pickups for his drug operation. He paid us well, so I guess I wasn't going to complain about the shit. I was saving all the money I could, I wanted to open up my tattoo shop down on South Street.

I was the man when it came to my artwork and tattooing, and these niggas were paying because my work wasn't cheap. This drug shit was just a way to make fast money to get what I wanted quicker. Love always talks shit about me going to college, and that shit just wasn't for me. I helped her with school because I knew her grandmother didn't have much. What she didn't get in scholarships I paid, and it would always be that way until she walked out of those doors as a pharmacist.

It took us about an hour to get to my pops' crib, Sin rang the doorbell and Cassy opened the door. Cassy was my dad's girl, and she wasn't shit! She was always on our dick when he wasn't around. I tried to tell his ass; that shit went in one ear and out the other. She gave us the same reaction as all the ladies did. I think we both loved the attention. Sin and I were blessed in the looks department and as we got older we perfected that shit, by working out and taking care of ourselves.

Our mother Naomi played no games about her sons, her ass was always on go! We used that shit to our advantage at times, especially when we wanted to get rid of a chick.

"Where Jax at?" Sin asked Cassy.

"He in his office," she said licking her lips.

"This bitch," I shook my head and walked off.

"Pop what's up?" I questioned as we walked into his office.

"That nigga Tron is what's up! I want my damn money and if that nigga ain't got my bread. Y'all need to handle that shit!" he yelled.

"How is this shit even our problem?" I asked him, getting irritated. My job was to drop off and pick up! If that nigga calling him saying he doesn't have his money he has men to handle shit like that.

"It's your problem because I just made it your problem! Now go get my fucking money!" he yelled jumping up from his desk.

"Let's get one thing straight, I'm your son and I know that! I'm also a man, and don't yo' ass forget that! Don't fucking come at me like that again, and I mean that shit. If we have to go hard on this nigga that owes you, then we get paid for that shit! Ain't shit free out this muthafucka but air and opportunity," I looked at his ass.

"Jax, if you want us to do the job, then we get paid for the job," Sin spoke standing up.

"Fine, now get the fuck out, and get my fuckin money!" he spoke and sat back in his chair. I turned and walked out of his office; my pop was an asshole. But he must have forgotten that I was a part of his bloodline. I'm not with the bullshit, they don't call me Law for nothing. I will break his fuckin' jaw when it's concerning me or my brother. Fuck that nigga, we ain't that fucking close.

"Let's just get this shit over with," I told Sin, as we jumped in the car and headed out west Philly to see this nigga, Tron. We walked inside the trap; Tron was seated at the table with some bitch on his lap.

"Nigga, where is Jax's money?" Sin asked him.

"I told Jax, I would get the fucking money when I get it! Who the fuck y'all supposed to be coming up in my shit like y'all running some shit!" This nigga stated, while his bitch ass crew laughed at his statement. They thought the shit was funny, but in a few minutes, we will see who would be laughing.

"Nigga do you have the money or not? Fuck what the hell you talking 'bout!" I spoke, ready to off this disrespectful ass nigga!

"Pussy, you heard me say I didn't fuckin'—" He was stopped in his tracks when my bullet pierced his bitch ass head. I pulled my shit so quick none of these pussies saw it coming. This nigga from his crew tried to pull his shit out and Sin put that nigga to sleep instantly. No one else made a move, I guess these niggas underestimated our fucking gangsta. I didn't need a crowd of niggas around me for me to make myself fuckin' clear.

"Where is the fucking money!" I yelled.

"He keeps everything in the back!" this dude spoke the hell up. Sin pushed his ass to the back with him and I kept my eyes on the other three niggas that were left in the room. These niggas were some true bitches, I know for a fact if I was in their shoes. I would be fighting my way out this bitch, fuck that! It was just me and Sin and only one nigga tried us, and his ass is dead. Sin and the dude came from the back each with three duffle bags in their possession.

"Stay right here until we get this shit in the car," Sin spoke. I laughed at Sin because this nigga wasn't playing, he had a duffle bag on each shoulder, a gun in one hand, and a duffle in the other.

"Do your thang, bro," I told him. About five minutes later, they both walked back in and Sin looked over at me.

"If any of you niggas think about fucking with us, just know I'm going to kill you and then I'm coming for the most important thing in your life! Your damn family," I spoke. Sin and I walked out and jumped in our car.

"Bruh, you are not going to believe this bullshit! Let's go to my house right the fuck now!" he spoke excitedly. When we finally made it to Sin's crib, we jumped out the car grabbing all of the duffle bags out of the trunk. He moved all the shit off the table, and we dumped all the money from the bags out.

"Bruh, how much did Tron owe Jax?" Sin questioned.

"Fifty G's," I told him.

"Law, this nigga kept all of his money in his trap. This dumb ass nigga never moved the money to a stash house. That trap was his stash house, I killed the nigga that guarded that room. Get comfortable bruh, it is going to be a long night," he stated. We ordered food and pulled out the counting machines and got busy. It was damn near ten the next morning by the time we were done counting and we were both sitting here staring at each other. This nigga had damn near seven million in that damn house and about twenty bricks.

"Bruh, you know what the fuck this means right?" Sin questioned.

"Man, this shit is fucking crazy, we need to pay pops his bread. I'm giving him double what he was owed; I will just tell him we collected interest. I' m giving you a year to help you start your own shit and then I'm out. We split the money down the middle after we get the product we need. I get thirty percent of this new empire we about to form. The rest is yours, and you will run that shit; I'm playing the back on this one," I said to Sin.

"Deal let's get this fucking money! I want you to live out your dreams, once we figure this shit out, you can go do you. We have enough bread here for you to get that building on South street that you wanted. Let's get some sleep and later we will make moves to put all this shit in motion," Sin stated, and we packed all the money up. He had a safe in the basement, so we decided to put it there until we were able to move it.

"Tomorrow we need to find another location to put this money," I told him because this basement shit wasn't going to work. We would be just as dumb as Tron was if we left it here.

"We need to stay strapped at all times, you never know what might happen since we made that move on Tron and his crew last night." He turned to walk out, and I followed behind him. I needed a hot shower, and some damn sleep. I can't believe we came up the way we did. Soon I was going to be able to put this street life behind me and open my first shop.

Chapter Three

SIN

My phone ringing jolted me out of my sleep. It was damn near dark outside. I grabbed my phone and it was Taj's ass calling again.

"What?!" I yelled on the phone. I was tired of her ass calling me.

"Sin, why the fuck are you doing this shit to me? You know damn well I didn't mean that shit. I told you I was drunk, and I wasn't thinking straight," she cried.

"Bitch, you were in the nigga's car fucking the hell out of him! So, what you just accidentally fell on the nigga dick?" I roared. Taj was a hoe, and I fell for the bullshit she was spittin' when we first met. I decided to stop by her crib on a surprise tip and there was a car parked in her driveway that didn't belong to her ass. Walking up the driveway you could hear screaming and moaning coming from that muthafucka.

What really took me out was, when the bitch started rocking. I peeped in the damn window, and Taj's ass was going for broke on that nigga's dick. I tapped on the window to get their attention, once she saw me. I headed back to my car and pulled the fuck off. There was no need to fuck the dude up, that bitch knew what it was. Besides, she was free to fuck who she wanted; she just wasn't gonna fuck me no damn more! Fuck her hoe ass!

"Sin, it just happened!" she yelled.

"Taj stop calling my fucking phone! If you call me again, I'm telling my fucking mama and we both know you don't want Naomi on that ass!" I hung up in that bitch's face; there was nothing else we needed to discuss. I looked down and her dumb ass was calling me again! I picked my phone up and dialed my mom.

"Hey handsome," my mom answered on the first ring.

"Ma, I caught Taj fucking this dude in his car. I told her to leave me the fuck alone, but she keeps fucking with me!" I smiled because I knew my mom was going to snap.

"I don't know how many times I have to tell you and your brother to leave these cum-bucket hoes alone! But noooooo, anything with a small waist and a fat ass, you two crusty ass niggas always trying to stick yo' dick in it! One day y'all gonna fuck around and that lil' shit in yo' pants gone fall the fuck off! I'm gone laugh at yo' no dick having asses too!" my mom fussed.

"Ma why my dick gotta be little? I'm blessed lil' mama. God did your boy right! You should be proud," I laughed.

"Nigga shut yo' mama's boy ass up and send me the address!" she yelled and hung up. My mother was forty-four years old, she had me when she was nineteen and Law when she was twenty-two. I swear our mother didn't look a day over twenty-five, and she was about that muthafuckin' life. Law and I had so much fun with her, in our eyes, she was the funniest thing to ever walk the face of this earth. It almost felt like she was our sister verses being our mom. But don't get that shit twisted, she reminded us every day that she was our mother.

We loved that lady to death; if a nigga ever fucked with Naomi Williams his ass was gonna die! I sent my mom Taj's address and told her to text me when she was on her way over there. There was no way I was going to miss this shit. I hopped up and went to take care of my hygiene. By the time I was dressed, Law was in the kitchen pulling food out of a bag.

"My nigga! I'm hungry as hell, this is love right here," I grabbed me a plate and piled it up with food.

"Yo' ass ain't never got shit in here to eat! You should tell Ma to go shopping for you and get some damn food in this place," Law stated.

"Nigga, I'm not getting cursed out asking Ma to do no damn shopping for me," I laughed, and he shrugged.

"Fuck it! Ma shops for me every Saturday and she cooks me food for the week. You do what you want, I just thought I would offer you some damn advice!" Law responded.

"Damn, how much you pay her?" I questioned because I know our mom ain't doing that shit for free.

"Five hundred a week," he replied.

"Bet, I'm about to go over to Taj's crib. She kept fucking with me, so I called mom on her," I told Law, and this nigga jumped up quick as hell.

"Nigga let's go; I don't want to miss this shit!" he stated. We went down to the basement and got the money that we would give Jax and left the house. About twenty minutes later we were sitting across the street from Taj's house. I had already got the text from mom that she was on her way over there. A few minutes went by, and a car came speeding down the street. Mom slammed on the breaks so damn hard. I thought her ass was going to come flying out of the wind-shield. She parked her car in the middle of the damn street like she owned the muthafucka!

"Mom is gonna fuck that damn Mercedes up, maybe we should have gotten her ass a Nissan," Law spoke, and I laughed. I rolled the windows down so we could hear the commotion. Taj swung the door open, and Naomi beat the breaks off of her ass right there in the door.

"Don't fuck with my son, bitch! The next time I come over here, I won't be so damn nice! You out here being a damn hoe and trying to give my son that nasty trash ass pussy! When you see him bitch you better walk on the other side of the street. Don't say shit to him, and don't call his damn phone!" Mom yelled and walked back to her car and pulled off. Law jumped out the car and walked up to the door where Taj was sitting still trying to get herself together. We always had to give that talk to whoever our mom fucked up. They needed to know what would happen if trouble came her way. Law got back in the car and I pulled off, headed to see Jax.

"Damn, y'all got my damn money and killed that nigga! That's what the fuck I'm talking about!" Jax spoke.

"Yeah, now give us our money so we can be out," Law said to him, as he stood up.

"I will give it to you later, I need to figure some shit out first," Jax stated, and I was pissed the fuck off. He stayed trying us over our fucking money!

"No nigga you gone give us our shit right now!" Law roared; I knew my brother was ready to fuck his pops up. But I had some shit that was way better than us getting that little bit of bread.

"We're done! You always fucking with us over our money. I'm not working for your ass no more," I told him.

"You might be done, but my son will always be with his pop!" Jax laughed.

"Nahhh nigga, I'm going to always be with my brother! If he's done; then I'm done, keep that fucking money you need it more than we do! Any other nigga would be dead right now, but since you my pop I'm just gone walk away from your grimy ass!" Law told him and walked out the door.

"You two niggas will be back! You broke niggas will need some money soon enough!" Jax roared, and I smiled. When we got back in the car, I looked at my brother. His veins were protruding out the side of his neck, he was so pissed.

"I just texted Zeno, Steve, and Cam to meet us at Onyx; it's time to shake some shit up!" I spoke and Law pulled off. It took us about thirty minutes to get to the club, and it was fucking packed. I got us a VIP section so we could drink and chill.

"What's up Law?" this chick name Saniya spoke.

"What's up? I will talk with you later. Make sure you chill out until I'm done handling this business," Law said to her. One thing about my brother and me, the ladies loved our asses and we ate that shit the hell up. There was never a shortage of women, I kept them in rotation. When Zeno, Steve, and Cam showed up we got down to business.

"Law and I are trying to branch out and do our own thing in this drug game. We wanted y'all to be on our team and get this money with us. Zeno, you already know you the problem solver. Cam and Steve, I need you two to build a street team of hittas to move this weight," I told them.

"Y'all already know I'm down," Zeno responded, and so did the rest of the guys. We agreed that we would meet in a few days, once the team was put together. I'm tired of being under Jax slimy ass, not making no real bread. I'm twenty-five years old, it was time to move up in this game and make some real money. For the rest of the night we partied. It was our time to shine.

Chapter Four
LOVE

It was the morning of graduation and Zion, and I was having breakfast. We wanted to spend some time together before we went our separate ways with our family and friends.

"You ready for the draft?" I smiled at him.

"Yeah, I'm ready, I'm praying I get picked up," he sighed.

"Zi, you will get picked up, you have to claim that shit. You got this, and I will be cheering you on." I kissed his cheek.

"Wherever I go, I want you to come with me," he pulled me closer to him.

"I plan on going to medical school, I have to focus on that," I told him.

"You can go to medical school anywhere; I'm not stopping

you from achieving your goals. I'm just saying you can achieve your goals with me," Zi replied.

"Zion, we don't even have a title to whatever we have going on right now," I stated.

"That can change right now, I want you Love, I need you in my life," he spoke, as he leaned over latching on to my lips. I broke the kiss, trying to stop my head from spinning in a million directions.

"I would have to think about this, I can't just jump and say yes. But I promise I will think about it," I spoke. A few minutes later we left and headed back to the dorms. It was time to start getting ready for our big day.

"Love who was that fine ass dude that stopped by the other day?" Erica asked while we were getting ready for graduation.

"That was my best friend, Law," I responded as I applied my makeup.

"Girl, that nigga was so fucking fine! You have to introduce us. Is he coming to graduation?" she questioned.

"Yeah, he will be here," I replied.

"Oh, hell yeah, let me put my best thong on. You never know his ass might be taking them off tonight!" she stated. I shook my head at her because she wasn't even Law's type of girl, she didn't have enough ass for him. The graduation had started, and they were giving out the degrees, I couldn't wait to get my degree in my hands.

"Love Stevenson," the Dean announced, and I stood. I

could hear Law, Sin, and my friends from school screaming and cheering me on. I hate that my cousin Tay couldn't make it, she had to work and couldn't take off. About an hour later, my graduation was over, and I was so damn excited. I already had my things packed up and ready to go. Once we graduated, we only had a certain amount of time to get our belongings out of the dorms. I decided that I would pack up and move out this weekend. I couldn't wait to get back to the city, because Law was throwing me a graduation party tonight. I walked through the crowd trying to find my grandmother, Law, and Sin.

"Love!" I heard someone yelling my name, I turned, and Law was standing there.

"Hey, best!" I screamed as I ran up to give him a hug.

"Congratulations, love bug!" He smiled at me.

"Thank you so much! If it wasn't for you, I don't know if this all would be possible," I said kissing him on his cheek.

"This was all you baby girl, now let's go celebrate this shit!" Law laughed.

"Baby, I'm so proud of you!" my Grammy cried.

"Grammy, don't cry," I told her.

"These are tears of joy, all I ever wanted was for you to make something of yourself. Congratulations baby," she said, as we hugged and shed some tears together. All those long talks and crying about how she was going to get the money to pay for my schooling. Then one day Law came over and talked to both of us. Letting us know that he would help us out, I could never repay him for what he has done for me and Grammy.

"I guess you couldn't find my mom, huh?" I looked at my Grammy.

"No baby, I tried, but we couldn't find her," she responded.

"No worries, it's her loss, not ours," I spoke.

"Yeah sis, congrats to you! We all proud of you," Sin stated, as I heard someone calling my name. Erica and Zion were walking up, they greeted everyone.

"Law, Grammy, and Sin this is my roommate Erica, and you all met Zion already."

"What's up," Law said to E and he ignored Zion. Zi pulled me in for a hug, as I smiled at him.

"I'm going to miss you, make sure you call me and remember what we talked about," he said and kissed my lips.

"I will," is all I said. When I turned to join my family, Law was putting E's number in his phone, and cutting his eyes at Zion. I didn't think she was his type, but I guess I was wrong.

"I need to grab my things and then we can leave," I told them and walked off with Erica. When I made it back outside, they were parked in front of the building. We had to make a few trips to get the rest of my belongings. Once we had everything in the trunk, we were on our way back to Philly. I'm going to miss seeing Zion, we already made plans that I would come out and visit him soon. He was leaving for Los Angeles later today. The NBA draft was a week away, and he had to get prepared for that.

Law took us to Ruth Chris for a late lunch, we were now on our way to drop my grandmother off at home. I was going to chill at Law's apartment until it was time for the party.

"Grammy I will see you later tonight, or in the morning if it's too late," I said to her.

"Okay, baby, y'all have a good time tonight, and be careful out there," she replied.

"It was good seeing you, Ms. Josephine!" Law yelled out.

"You as well, Law, stop by and see me sometimes," she told him, and Sin helped her into the house. About twenty minutes later, we pulled up to Law's apartment building on City Ave. Sin hopped into his car and pulled out of the parking space.

"I will see y'all tonight!" he yelled out.

"See you tonight, bro," Law responded, holding the door for me to walk in. I have never been to his new place. He moved here a few months ago.

"Best this is really nice, you did good!" I looked at him and smiled. I walked through the apartment; he had three bedrooms and two full bathrooms. The master bedroom was big as hell, and damn did his king-size bed look comfortable. I slipped my shoes off and jumped right in his shit.

"What the hell are you doing?" he asked.

"I'm about to get comfortable and take a nap, boo boo," I laughed.

"Nah, you better take yo' ass in there and pick out your bedroom and nap in that muthafucka," his serious expression let me know he wanted me out of his bed. But I was staying right here, we have slept in the same bed plenty of times.

"Bye boy, I'm sleeping right here," I spoke, as I got out of the bed and grabbed a tank top out of my bag. I slipped my dress off and slid my tank top on and hopped right back in the bed. I didn't care about Law seeing me half naked.

"So, you just gone sleep in my bed with all that ass in my face, huh?" he asked.

"Yup," I giggled. He grabbed me and began tickling me, I was laughing so damn hard I could barely catch my breath.

"Why are you playing with me, L?" he asked, and the look on his face was something that I have never seen before.

"What's wrong, what did I do?" I questioned, as I tried to sit up. But he pushed me back down and crashed his lips into mine. At first, I was caught off guard, but it felt so good I immediately latched onto his bottom lip and began sucking the hell out of it. The kiss was so damn intense neither of us thought about what we were doing. I came back to my senses and pushed him away.

"What are we doing?" I asked him.

"What I have been wanting to do for a long damn time," he stated, as he bent down and began sucking and licking on my neck and chest. We fought to remove the little bit of clothing we had on. He stared at me with hunger in his eyes, I couldn't look away even if I wanted too.

"You know this will change everything for us. But I can't fucking help it, I want to bury myself inside of you so fucking bad, my heart aches," he gritted out. I wrapped my arms around his neck pulling him back in for a kiss, the kiss was so damn good and erotic. I felt his finger slide up and down my slit, I arched my back from the sensation. A few seconds later, he was licking and sucking on my pearl and I thought I was going to lose my entire mind.

He was skilled at eating pussy that's for sure. I dug my fingernails in his back trying to hold on for dear life. I lifted my body from the bed as he gripped my ass to hold me steady, it felt like he was trying to suck my soul out of my body. The moans were uncontrollable, and I felt the urge in the bottom of my stomach. I was about to cum, and I was going to cum in his mouth if he didn't move out the way.

"Law, I'm cumming. Shit you have to move, I can't ahhhh-hhh.....I can't hold it," I screamed, as soon as I started cumming. He jumped up as he eased inside of me, giving deep strokes.

"Oh my God!" I screamed out. I wasn't a virgin, but I fucking felt like it right now. He was so fucking big, it felt like he would split me in two.

"Fuck!" He gritted as he thrust deeper into me.

"Lawwww! Fuck, I can't take it," I moaned, as he continued to fuck the shit out of me.

"Love, you can handle this baby! Ahhhhhhhhhhhh shit! This muthafucka sooooo damn good," he growled. He pulled out of me and flipped me over and slammed back inside of me. All you could hear was the sound of us going for broke. He pulled out and laid down for me to ride him and I swear that nigga fucked my whole life up! I was supposed to be riding him, but I lost the battle.

"I'm cumming! Fuck, I'm cumming!" I screamed as tears were flowing down my face.

"Fucking with me, that's all your fine ass is going to be doing! Let that shit go, Love bug! Urggghhhh," he growled, as he went deeper, and deeper until he released so hard in me, I felt fluids splashing against my walls.

"Love bug, are you okay?" he asked looking at me. I always knew that Law was a nice-looking man. I'm looking at him now, and he was just too damn fine! His damn body was insane, the muscles and tattoos everywhere just made his ass a work of art.

"I'm fine. Law, what just happened?" I questioned. I'm not sure how to feel about what we just did.

"We just fucking discovered how bad we wanted each other. How good it felt being connected in that way. I don't know what will happen next, but I love you too much to fuck up our friendship. I'm sorry, Love, but I have been fighting this battle about you in my head and my heart for a year now. A fucking year, Love bug and having you in my bed like this. Something just took over me, and I couldn't stop it. Fuck it, I didn't want to stop it," Law said, as he pulled me into him and eased his tongue in my mouth. For the next couple of hours, we were fucking each other like our lives depended on that shit. *What the fuck did we just get ourselves into?!*

Chapter Five

LAW

There was no way that I could fight my feelings for Love any longer. Now that I have been inside of her and felt her fucking pussy, and how that shit gripped me up! There was no way that I was going back to us just being best friends. We were sitting in VIP at this new club LIT that opened up a few months ago. We rented the club out and invited the whole hood out to celebrate with Love. Lil' Baby & Gunna *Drip Too Hard* was blasting through the speakers. Just watching Love gyrate her body had me in my damn feelings.

These niggas were on her ass hard tonight, Love was a beautiful girl and her body was fucking sick! I mean everything was just right on her, she had wide hips, and her ass was fucking amazing. She was a shade of caramel with the most beautiful brown eyes I have ever seen on a woman. I always knew she was fine, and the niggas were always on her top. But tonight, it was different, she belonged to me and I would kill every nigga in this muthafucka over her. I walked over to her and pinned her against the railing.

"I think you need to come sit down with me, don't cause a murder scene in this bitch!" I whispered in her ear.

"Why? They just looking, they can't have me," she smiled as she grazed my neck with her tongue.

"I'm going to pour me another drink," she said and walked off.

"Nigga tell me you didn't! Please tell me you didn't slide up in Love?!" Sin questioned.

"Okay, I didn't," I responded, as I watched Love sip on her drink.

"You a whole muthafuckin lie! Ma gone fuck you up, she told you not to go there with Love! That best friend and sex shit don't work nigga! I can't wait to call ma and tell her this shit!" He went on, and on. I was about to respond to his snitching ass when gunshots rang out. We instantly pulled our guns out letting that shit rip. Love was down on the floor screaming and crying, I moved over to her quickly trying to get her to safety.

"Come on, we have to get out of here!" Sin yelled. The club had an emergency side door exit, and we moved out through those doors.

"What the fuck! This was a private fucking party, who would come in and try to get at us?" I roared.

"I think that was some of Tron's crew," Sin spoke.

"This is why I told y'all you need to leave this drug shit alone! We could have been killed, and for fucking what?! All because you want to make some quick fucking money!" Love yelled.

"Love this is not the time for this bullshit, that quick money is what helped pay for your college education. I got shit that I need to do, and this is what I'm going to do right now to get that shit! Let me get you out of here, we can discuss this shit later," I told her, now was not the time for her to give us a damn lecture about being in the game.

"So, you not gone stop, until one of you are dead?!" she cried.

"I have a plan, and I will be in this game until my plan comes together!" I yelled, and she turned away from me.

"Zeno, can you take me home, please?" she asked him.

"Love, I will take you home," I said to her, as I pulled her into me. She snatched away and walked off, I nodded to Zeno for him to take her home. I will check on her tomorrow after she cools down, right now I got some niggas to murder.

"Yo, one of the niggas that we hit was definitely one of Tron guys," Cam spoke walking up to us. We need to get out of here because the cops were called.

"We need to get back on they ass tonight!" I told them. I was fucking pissed; Love was right shit could have gone bad for us tonight. Steve pulled up in his truck and we all jumped in.

"Is everybody strapped?" Sin asked.

"Let's go, I want to end this shit right now." I was fucking irritated and this shit Love was spittin' was weighing heavy on my ass. I have never seen her blow up on me like she did tonight. Hell, we have never been in this type of situation and I know that she was scared out of her mind. We pulled down the street from Tron's trap and jumped out of the car.

There was no need for us to talk this shit through. I walked up on the porch with the guys trailing me and we could hear them inside celebrating. Talking shit about what they did to us, the dumbest shit ever was to come back to this trap, after you tried to take us out! I kicked the door in and began blasting off on they ass. We damn sure caught them niggas off guard and that's the way I wanted that shit to be.

Once every nigga in here was dead. We turned and left the same way we came in; I had no time for bullshit with any of these street niggas! You come for me; I'm dropping yo' ass! I decided to head home and calm the fuck down. When I was pissed the fuck off, it was hard as hell to bring me back down. I thought today was gonna be the start of something beautiful with Love. I'm not too sure about that now, she was extremely pissed with me. The next day I went over to Ms. Josephine's house to see Love. I knocked on the door and waited for someone to answer.

"Hey, Law, how you doing?" Ms. Josephine asked when she opened the door.

"I'm good, how are you?" I questioned.

"Oh baby, I'm blessed by the best! If you came to see Love, that child left here this morning saying she was going to California. She went out there with that boyfriend of hers, she said she didn't know when she would be back," Ms. Josephine stated, and that shit damn near knocked the air out of my body.

"Okay, well if you hear from her can you please let her know to call me?" I told her and walked back to my car. Once inside, I immediately dialed Love's phone and her voicemail picked up. *What the fuck!*

Chapter Six

SIN

a week had passed, and it was pretty quiet since we took care of that shit with Tron's crew. Law and I had already started setting up shop to get this drug game on lock. My brother really didn't want to be a part of this business and I truly wanted him to open up his shop. We found the perfect spot on South Street for his Tattoo shop and that shit was going to be fya! Law was hell with putting that ink on yo' ass! His clients were just as excited as we were about our plans to open. This nigga got all the rappers and shit hittin' him up to tat them up.

"Sin, are we going to lunch?" Diamond asked as she rolled over to face me.

"Yeah, we can do that, but first I need to slide up in that pussy one more time," I said to her as I kissed her lips. Diamond and I have been seeing each other for a couple of weeks, she was different than what I was accustomed to fucking with. I hovered over her as I sheathed my dick with the condom.

"Uhhh shit, stop playing with me and give me the dick," she moaned as I slid my index finger up and down her pussy lips. I eased inside of her giving her ass death strokes, and that shit was driving her ass crazy.

"Shit, that's right, fuck me with that big dick!" she screamed out as she met me thrust for thrust. Diamond was so damn mild-mannered until you got her ass between the sheets. She was a lil' damn freak, and I was loving that shit.

"Damn!" I gritted; the pussy was decent but not the best I've had. She was in the top five though. I continued to go deeper, and deeper inside of her. Our skin slapping against each other was all you could hear, besides her moans.

"Ohhhh shit Sin! I'm cumming!" she moaned.

"Mmmm hmmmm I with you lil' mama!" I gritted as I filled my condom up, and she came with me. After we were dressed, Diamond and I went to lunch before she left to go home. The boys and I were getting together in a couple of hours to watch the NBA draft at my house. By the time I got back home, I had to order the food for tonight, and make sure the bar was stocked.

A couple of hours later, Cam, Steve, and Law had made it, and everybody was just hanging out and talking shit. Law was a little down because Love had left town with that nigga from her school. She could have at least talked to bro, before she just up and left like that. Maybe she was just going away for the week since ol' boy was supposed to be in the draft.

"Yo, turn that up!" Law yelled out. The commentators were talking, and they had Zion's name on the screen.

"Jeff, Zion Hill is the number one pick on a lot of teams' radar tonight! It is believed that the Miami Heat organization is up next, and they will be selecting Zion Hill," the news commentator stated.

"Mike, you can almost bet that Miami will grab him up! Zion is here tonight with his parents, and his new wife, Love Hill. It has been reported that Zion and his college sweetheart were married yesterday in a private ceremony here in Los Angeles," the reporter said, and I looked over at my brother. Law looked as if he was ready to blow the fuck up, as he watched them talk about Hill, and Love as they showed the two of them on the screen.

"This fucking bitch! Are you fucking serious?! She went and married this pussy ass nigga?!" Law roared. I have never heard him talk that way about Love ever.

"Bro calm down there is nothing we can do about it! She made the fucked-up decision to marry this nigga, and that's what it is. She will come around and talk to you about it, it's Love. You two have been best friends for a long ass time. Just give her time to get her thoughts together. She will call you," I told him.

"Fuck that and fuck her!" Law yelled as he went into an all-out rage! Throwing and breaking up my shit. I sent out a text and then tried to calm this nigga down, but there was no stopping him. I would have to shoot this husky ass nigga, just to slow him down! I would rather him just tear my shit up, and he pays to get my place back in order.

"What the fuck is going on in hear? Savion what the fuck is wrong with you?" my mom yelled at Law. I knew she was pissed because she always called out our government when she was mad.

"Fuck her, Ma! Fuck that bitch!" Law roared.

"Fuck what bitch? Who fucking with you, son? Because we can go handle this shit right the fuck now!" my mom said to him.

"Mom, he is talking about Love," I told her, and she turned and smacked the shit out of my bro.

"Why the fuck are you calling Love out of her name, disrespecting her like that!" she yelled at him.

"Fuck her, she went and married that nigga!" Law roared.

"Awww, Love got married! Why didn't she invite us to the wedding, and why the fuck are you so pissed about it?" Ma asked Law and then it hit her, and she began to hit his ass.

"What are you hitting me for?" he questioned.

"You better tell me you didn't stick that lil' piece of a dick you got in Love! I told your punk ass not to fuck that girl, but you fucked her, didn't you? I told you it would fuck up y'all friendship! Now, look at you, sitting here looking like a lost fucking dickless duck! Get yo' ass up and come the fuck on, you gone fix your brother shit too," our mother fussed. Law got up and went with her because fighting with her would be a mistake. I guess he would be staying with mom until she thinks he is calm enough to go back home. When they left Steve, Cam, and I burst into a fit of laughter.

"Yooo, Ms. Naomi don't play with y'all ass at all! My mom wouldn't have given a fuck about my black ass out here spazzing the fuck out," Cam stated.

"Yeah, that nigga in trouble, but Ma gotta stop putting our ass on punishment when we act up. I'mma tell her ass that shit, we the hell grown now! Nahhhh, I ain't telling her shit, I will go check on that nigga tomorrow. Y'all help me clean this shit up." We laughed and began cleaning up the mess my brother made. I know this bullshit fucked my brother up, finding out that Love had gotten married. It's time that he focused on what's important and that's getting his business up and running.

I have to get my mind right my damn self; we have a very important meeting tomorrow. I got hooked up with a drug connect and I'm praying he agrees to work with us. But I need to get Law back on track before that meeting takes place. My brother can be a damn live wire at times, and we don't need shit fucking up this meeting.

The next morning, I went over to my mother's house to check on Law. I could hear my mom on the phone talking, so I walked into her family room.

"Hey ma," I spoke as I kissed her on the cheek.

"Carla, let me call you back. My son just walked in and I need to talk to him," my mother said to her best friend.

"Hey son, your brother is up in his room still in his damn feelings. I told his ass he couldn't get mad because Love chose somebody else. That's a part of life, you get some ass and then you lose some! Didn't nobody tell his ass to go dipping in the love pot any damn way," my mom was crazy as hell. I was bent over laughing at her ass because she was definitely certified.

"Mom, you are too much. I guess I need to go up and check on him because I need him to get his mind right," I said to her.

"You know I'm going on a cruise with Jax, we leave on Saturday," she spoke, and I was heated.

"Mom, why do you keep messing with this nigga! I know he is Law's dad but he ain't shit! You already know he ain't shit, and yet you keep fucking with him!" I yelled because I was pissed that she keeps dealing with this piece of shit ass nigga!

"Watch your damn mouth when you talking to me! You don't have to tell me what kind of man Jax is, I have been dealing with him for twenty-three years. I'm comfortable with my position, and until I'm ready to move on I will continue to mind my business and yours too. The shit between us just works, and I'm fine with that! Just as long as he never disrespects me," she stated, and I just walked off because she sounds crazy as hell right now. I went upstairs to check on Law, I knocked on the door and he didn't say anything. So, I just walked in and he was lying across the bed.

"What up!" I spoke.

"My bad about your crib last night. I will replace your stuff, just let me know what I fucked up," he stated.

"Have you talked to her?" I asked him.

"She keeps sending me to voicemail," he responded. I decided to try my luck and pray this didn't blow out of proportion. I pulled my phone out and dialed Love's number, just to see if she would pick up for me.

"Hello," she picked up on the first ring.

"Love, what in the hell did you do?" I asked her and Law stood up. I put my hand up to stop him because we needed to understand why she left and married this guy.

"I left because I couldn't get through to you two. Especially Law, we have had the same talk for years, Sin. This drug game can be dangerous and that night at my party opened my eyes. I don't want to be around that type of mess, I don't want you two to be involved in that type of shit. I love you both too much to see you hurt, or dead and Law just disregarded my feelings about it," Love cried.

"So, your feelings is all that fucking matters! It was okay when I was spending that same drug money on clothes, food, and college tuition for you. Better yet it was okay when I was helping your grandmother out with bills. The shit only matters now because you were at the forefront of it all! On top of all that, you let me fuck you and a week later you go fucking marry this nigga! Why because he can take care of you now, and you don't need me anymore! You one selfish ass chick, fuck you, Love!" Law yelled and walked out. When I looked at the phone, she had hung up. I don't think we will hear from her no time soon; I hope he can get over this shit.

"Bruh, pull yourself together we have that meeting with

the connect in a few hours," I told him as I walked out on the deck where he was sitting.

"I'm cool, I will be ready," he responded. I decided not to talk to him about mom and Jax right now. That would only make matters worse, he hated their relationship just as much as I did. I decided to stay at my mom's and chill until it was time to head out. A few hours later we pulled up to this warehouse, out in the county to meet with the new connect. I thought it was best that we arrived early just so he could see that we meant business. I knocked on the door and waited for someone to come and let us in. A few minutes later a big husky nigga answered the door.

"What you want?" he asked.

"What we want is for your big ass to move, and let Tee know we're here," I told him. He stepped to the side and let us in.

"Sin, Law, come on in and let's talk," this bad ass chick stated.

"If you don't mind, I would rather talk to Tee in person," I told her.

"I am Tee, now sit your ass down and let's talk. You think because I'm a woman I'm not supposed to be the one in charge?" she questioned.

"Lil' mama, I was thrown off a little, but before we get started watch how you address me. I will give you the same amount of respect you give me!" I told her, she was fine and all but I'm not sure who the fuck she thought she was talking too.

"I thought we were supposed to be cool, what happened nigga? Chill the fuck out," Law whispered to me.

"Have a seat, or you can turn around and walk out that door! It doesn't really matter to me," this smart mouth ass girl spoke.

"Yo, let's just sit and hear her out," Law said. We both sat down in the chairs across from Tee, and some other chick that was sitting beside her.

"My price is sixteen a brick, we get paid when your shipment arrives," Tee said, and sat back in her chair.

"That's it?" Law asked, and I just stared at her. I can see that if we get into business together, me and Ms. Tee are going to bump heads.

"We need a hundred bricks, I will send you the address we need it delivered to," I told her, and I dropped a duffle bag on the table. You will get the rest when I get my product," I stated.

"That's what I like to hear, nice doing business with you, Sin! You will have your shipment tomorrow," Tee replied, as she held her hand out for me to shake it. I shook her hand, and we turned and walked out of the warehouse.

"Yo, what the hell was that all about in there?" Law questioned.

"That chick was a lil' too disrespectful for me, but we need the product so I'm good for now," I responded.

"Listen we got the product, now we need to get this shit moving," Law pointed out, and I had to agree. Now wasn't the time to let any bullshit get in the way of our plans. Right now, we were trying to make shit pop for us. It was hard as hell hustling on the corner and then moving up to picking up and dropping off Jax's money. That shit was paying but it wasn't paying us like that. We lucked up and lifted that money from Tron and his crew, which set us up for a major come up. Now we just have to make smart decisions, on what we do and how we do it. We gone also have to find a way to clean that money, so I need to work on that shit as well.

"Bruh, Tee was fucking fine," I looked over at him smiling.

"Indeed, she was, and she had your ass all messed up. But she seems like the type to give you a run for your money. So, if that's who you are going after, nigga you need to be ready for the chase," Law spoke as he got comfortable in his seat. I don't know about chasing her ass, I never had to do that shit! But I wouldn't mind seeing what was up with her.

Chapter Seven

LOVE

Almost Seven Years Later

My phone ringing jolted me out of my sleep. I looked at my clock and it was four in the morning. I saw that it was my grandmother calling, and I quickly answered the phone.

"Grammy, are you alright?" I questioned the minute I hit the answer button.

"Love, you need to come home, baby, it's your mother. They found her dead last night, she done overdosed on those drugs," my grandmother cried in the phone.

I never had a real relationship with my mother, I wasn't important enough to ever matter to her. But my heart always ached for her, and she was one of the reasons I wanted Law to not sell that shit. It was killing people, and I just couldn't be a part of that mess. Knowing that he was pushing that shit in the streets, the same drugs my mother was using. It damn near killed me when I walked away from him.

"What?! Grandma calm down and get some rest. I will be home as soon as I can. Is anyone there with you?" I asked her.

"No, but your aunt and cousin are on the way here now," she stated.

"Okay, I will get on the next flight out," I told her. We spoke for a few more minutes and then ended the call. I broke down and cried for my mother, there was nothing we could do to help her. Every time we tried to put her in rehab, she would always leave. It has been a year since I saw my Grammy last. I would always fly her out to Miami to see me, just so that I could avoid going back home to Philly.

There was no way for me to avoid this trip, I logged onto my iPad and booked two one-way tickets to Philadelphia. I had no idea when I was coming back, I would make that decision once I knew for sure. My ex-husband Zion, and I got a divorce a few years ago. He came to me one night saying that he thought we made a mistake by getting married. The real reason his bitch ass was coming to me, is that he had another woman. I knew Zion was cheating on me, and I just didn't care. We went through so much shit, with him putting his hands on me and just being disrespectful. I had my faults as well; I knew I shouldn't have married Zion. My heart just wasn't in it, and I think he knew that.

My heart has always belonged to one man, and it wasn't Zion. I was unable to let go of Savion Williams aka Law, I tried but I just couldn't do it. It has been almost six years since I have seen or talked to him, and I knew he would never forgive me for what I have done. We were rushing into the airport. Our flight was leaving at one, and it was 12:15 right now.

"Mommy why are we running so fast?" my son Savi spoke. I knew he was tired, but we had to at least make it through the security checkpoint.

"Come on baby, we are almost there," I urged. Once we made it through security, I picked him up and carried him to the gate. He was turning six in a couple of weeks, and he was so excited about his birthday. I struggled to get through school and having a child, but I did it. I have been a Pharmacist for the last couple of years and I love everything about my profession. I was awarded a great deal of money in my divorce settlement from Zion. I was thinking about using some of the money to open my own Pharmacy. I haven't decided if I would do it or not, it would take a lot of planning to pull that off. It was going on five in the evening by the time we pulled up in front of my grandmother's house.

"Come on, baby," I said to my son as I unbuckled his seatbelt and got him out of the car. The door was open, I heard everyone talking in the kitchen.

"Well praise God! My baby done made it home," my Grammy stated, getting up from her seat to give me a hug.

"Love, it sure is good to see you," my aunt Gerry said.

"Hey auntie, it is good seeing you, I missed you guys. Where is Tay?" I asked her.

"She is in the back, that child has been waiting on you to

get here," my aunt Gerry stated, just as my cousin Tay walked into the room.

"Yesss bihhhh, you are giving us all that Miami rich people swag!" Tay spoke, and we hugged.

"Hey Tay, it's good to see you," I told her.

"Whose little boy is this? Well look at all this little cuteness here, hey handsome," she said to Savi.

"My name is Savion Jaxon Williams Jr. not handsome," Savi told her and it was like the entire room went quiet.

"Ohhh well, it's nice to meet you Savion Jaxon Williams Jr. Grandma, you better hold on to your good wig, and black dress because it's going to be a double funeral for this family," Tay said, looking over at me and I was officially scared shitless.

"Love y'all go ahead and get situated in your bedroom," my grandmother said. I took Savi, and our luggage and got him settled in the room with his game and the television. I decided that I needed to go back out and face them, I knew I couldn't stay locked up in this room. When I walked out of the room, Tay was standing by the door.

"Bitch, all them damn phone conversations we had. Yo' ass forgot to mention that you gave birth to lil' Albert Einstein Jr. and shit!" Tay whispered. I knew she would be mad, but I didn't know how to tell her. We just kind of drifted away from each other, that was mainly my fault. The few times she did come to Miami. I either met her at her hotel or told her that I wouldn't be in town.

"I'm sorry, Tay. I was going through a lot, please don't hold this against me," I begged her.

"We're good, just don't do that shit again. We are always supposed to be there for each other, and you just blocked me out of your life," she said, and I felt so damn bad.

"I wanted to call you so many times and talk to you, but I just couldn't do it," I told her.

"L, does he know that you have his son?" she questioned, and I just nodded my answer to her. I was so fucking embarrassed that I did something like this. I even hid it from my grandmother for three years of his life. When she came to visit is when she found out about Savi, and I begged her not to say a word. She was against it, and she still is. Every time we spoke on the phone, she told me I needed to tell him. I knew I fucked up by staying away from my family and keeping Savi a secret. My grandmother said she only saw Law a few times in almost seven years. She said he would speak to her and asked was she alright. But he never asked her about me, and when she told me that, it hurt me to the core.

"Love, you have to tell him, this shit is wrong on so many fucking levels. Not only that, Law and his finnnnnnnneee ass brother stopped by here earlier. They wanted to know what Grammy needed, he said they would be dropping off food later today! I don't know what your ass is going to say to him, but bitch you better go practice that shit and come back and rehearse it with my ass!" Tay stated, and I was ready to get my son and go to a damn hotel.

Chapter Eight

LAW

*I*t was sad to hear about Ms. Evelyn passing. When Sin called me and told me what happened. I told him we had to go by and check on Ms. Josephine. I'm not sure where Love was these days. I did hear in the news that she divorced her husband for allegations of him cheating. I felt bad for her, but there wasn't much I could do about it. It has been damn near seven years and I still can't grasp the fact that we haven't talked or seen one another for that long. As the saying goes, time heals all wounds. Things have really changed in my life for the better. I now have ten tattoo shops that I own outright, and I've hired the best tattoo artists in the country.

Ink Drip is known for giving you some of the dopest ink you have ever seen. I personally work out of my Philadelphia location, and I stay booked. It's crazy how shit works out sometimes, I was so dope with my ink game. You have to book at least six months in advance just to get on my books. My shops are in Miami, Cali, Atlanta, New York, New Orleans, I have two in Philly, Las Vegas, Orlando, and Charlotte. My dreams became a reality and now I'm bringing in millions in this business along with my other businesses. I'm no longer in the drug game but I still get a percentage of what Sin brings in.

My brother is killing the game right now, and my pop is one pissed off nigga. He went off when he found out that Sin and I were moving dope in his city. We tried not to step on his toes, but that shit was bound to happen, and his ass eventually had to bow out gracefully. The team Sin built was a muthafuckin dream team. They were bringing in that fucking money by the boatload. In order to have peace between my pop and us, we decided to give his ass a small percentage to shut him the fuck up. I still don't believe he stopped his hustle; I just think he changed that shit up to make us believe he did. I tried to tell Sin that shit but he didn't want to hear it.

"Hey babe, is everything alright?" Shantel asked me.

"Yeah, I'm good, beautiful lady. Sin and I have to take this food over to Ms. Josephine's house in a few," I said to her.

"Ohhh did your little best friend come home?" Shan questioned.

"I'm not sure, but it is her mother so I'm sure she will be home at some point. Don't start your shit, Shan, you already know the deal with me and Love. You just worry about becoming my wife in a couple of weeks," I told her, as I kissed her lips. Shantel and I have been engaged for the last two years, and it was almost time for our wedding.

I loved everything about my fiancé. She was beautiful, intelligent, and loyal. I couldn't wait to marry her ass, and me possibly seeing Love wasn't going to change that. So, I'm not sure what she was worried about. I decided to tell Shantel about Love, I didn't want to keep anything from her. She knew the good, and bad parts of my life and I knew hers. I hated a liar, that shit was something that I despised with a fucking passion.

"I'm not worried, and the wedding details are all set. I'm hanging out with my girls, I will be in a little late tonight," Shantel stated, and walked out. I left out right behind her, when I got to the garage, I had to decide which car I was driving. I glanced over at the covered car in the corner. I walked over and pulled the cover off; after all these years she was still a beauty. I took some of that money we took from Tron that night and purchased the newest Bentley continental, and loaded it with gifts and money for Love on her graduation day.

I was going to give it to her the night of her graduation party but never got the chance to do it. I tried so many times to get rid of it, but I could never do it. I took it for a test drive around the block, and I kept the maintenance up. The car only has a couple thousand miles on it, I grabbed the keys from the wall and hopped in. I think it was time for me to turn it over to its rightful owner. If she decided to come home and was at her grandmother's, I could give it to her. I called Sin, to go pick the food up and meet me at Ms. Josephine's house.

By the time I pulled up there were so many people outside, laughing and talking. I see that Love's family all came together for Ms. Evelyn. In the past, these niggas were nowhere to be found. Ms. Josephine told me earlier that she did have life insurance on her daughter. I was ready to step up and help her if I needed to do that. I never asked her about Love, and what she had going on but I'm sure she could also afford to pay for her mother's funeral if she needed to do so. When I got out of the car, Sin pulled up in the middle of the street and popped his trunk. I called out for some of the men in the yard to come help take the food in the house.

"What's up, bro?" he asked.

"I was just about to walk inside when you pulled up," I told him.

"Remember, what we talked about. Keep your cool, it has been a long time and shit is different now," Sin reminded me.

"I'm good, if she is here, I just hope she is well. I wouldn't start anything with her, I'm sure she's going through a tough time with her mother's passing," I stated. We walked into the house with all of the food, and there were so many people inside. When we got back to the kitchen, Ms. Josephine, Ms. Gerry, Loves cousin Tay, and some other ladies were in there.

"Oh boys, I can't thank you two enough for all of this," Ms. Josephine cried, I walked up to give her a hug and handed her an envelope. Even though she had life insurance, I still wanted to help her in some way. Tay spoke to us and walked out of the room abruptly. A few minutes later, she came back and Love was behind her. My damn heart felt as if it was going to burst out of my chest. Time has definitely changed a lot of things. She was no college student anymore. This woman was absolutely fucking beautiful, and I might be wrong for thinking this, but damn she was fine as hell!

"Damn, lil' Love ain't little no more that heifer is fine fine," Sin whispered, as he jolted me out of the daze, I was in. She walked into the kitchen and Sin decided to speak first, I needed a moment to gather myself.

"L Boogie look at you girl! It's been a long time, I'm so sorry to hear about your mom," Sin said to her, and hugged her.

"Sin, thank you. It's good to see you, you still look the same," Love replied.

"Funny you say that, you don't look the same you grew up on us," Sin's dumb ass said.

"Yes, I have grown a little," she smiled and then turned her focus on me.

"Hey Law, it's good to see you," Love said to me. Damn, I thought I let this shit go, but looking at her just pissed me the fuck off.

"It's good to see you as well, I'm sorry to hear about Ms. Evelyn," I replied to her and excused myself from the room and walked out the door. The fire inside of me was rising and I didn't want that shit to blow up at a time like this. A few minutes later, Sin came out the house looking confused as hell.

"Nigga, really!" Sin spoke, as he walked up on me.

"Man, just seeing her pissed me the fuck off!" I spoke angrily.

"Well I guess this won't be a good reunion between you two, fuck it! Do you, bro, because I'm not about to be pulling on yo' ass to get you out of here. Fucking up my damn thousand-dollar shirt, I'm tired of you fucking up my shit over Love's ass. Just know I'm calling mom on your ass!" Sin stated, just as Love walked up.

"Excuse me, Law, can I speak to you for a moment in private?" she asked.

"Yeah, what's up?" I looked at her, waiting for her ass to say something.

"Law, I'm so sorry, for leaving the way I did. I was just so full of anger, I wanted better for you and I was afraid that something would happen to you," she cried.

"So, you thought it was best to leave because you were afraid, you thought I was going to die?" I questioned her.

"Yes, I did," she whispered.

"Well guess what, I died! I died when you left with that bullshit explanation you gave. Even though I walked around and did what I had to do. I made sure my livelihood was good, and my family was good. Even though I did all of that, I was dead inside, because you unapologetically slid a knife in my fucking heart!" I yelled, and I swear I didn't mean to bring this shit to her now. But damn, this girl just fucked our friend-ship up. That meant more to me than us fucking.

"I'm sorry," she burst into tears. I could only pull her into my chest and wrap my arms around her.

"I'm sorry, this is not the time for this shit. You need to focus on what's important and that's your mother's funeral. I do have something I need to give you before I get out of here," I told her, and she followed behind me. I walked up to the car and stopped in front of it.

"This was your graduation gift that I got for you. I was going to give it to you the night of the party. Shit popped off and I never had the chance to give it to you. I think it's time that I give it to its rightful owner," I said to her and handed her the keys.

"Savion, you bought me a Bentley?" she questioned smiling at me.

"I did, of course, it's damn near seven years old now, if you want it upgraded, I can do that for you. Just let me know," I told her as I gave her a hug and walked off to get in the car with Sin.

"Ummmm you do know you about to get married, right?" Sin questioned.

"I'm Gucci, let's ride," I told him and sat back in my seat. I think it's best that I stay away from Ms. Love, my heart should not be jumping around like that, at the sight of her. Damn!

Chapter Nine

SIN

I sure hope my brother knows what he's doing. The way he acted at Ms. Josephine's house with Love was a sure indication that he still had feelings for her.

"So, you saying he was over there acting a plum fool?" my mom asked.

"Well, not a plum fool but he damn sure was on one. When he saw her, it was like he was about to snap. Ion know ma, we may have to watch his ass. It seems that any little thing concerning Love can send him over the edge," I told her.

"I'm not going to say anything to him right now, but I will be watching from the sideline," Mom stated.

"Alright, I have to go. I will chat with you later, make sure you stop by and see Ms. Josephine," I said to her, and we ended the call. I got out the car and headed in the warehouse.

Ever since I got into business with Tee, shit has been smooth for my ass. She turned out to be a real cool person and damn did I want her ass.

I have been asking this girl out every damn month for fucking years. Each time I asked her out she would shoot me down, I decided not to ask anymore. She's obviously not interested, it's time to move on and maybe make shit pop with Meka. We have been fucking around for a few months, and we just haven't made a move to be in a relationship. But a nigga wasn't getting any younger and I think it was time to settle down. When I got inside, Tee's crew was inside getting my package together.

"Sin, you're early, they should have your package together soon," Tee said walking up to me.

"Cool, how are you?" I asked her.

"Life is good, what about you?" she questioned.

"No complaints, here is your bread," I told her as I dropped the duffle bags on the table. Her right-hand girl, Blue picked the money up and walked off.

"What's wrong, you not going to ask me out on a date?" she smiled.

"Nah, I'm good, I have been asking you out for a long ass time and each time you shut me down," I responded, looking in her eyes.

"Ask me again, Sin," she whispered.

"Why, so you can get joy out of saying NO?!" I questioned her.

"Ask me again," she stated.

"Teana, can a nigga take you out on a real date?" I looked at her, as a smile crept across her face.

"Yes, dinner at my house, I will cook for you," she stated.

"Wait, can you even cook?" I asked her.

"I guess you will have to wait and see, tomorrow night at seven. I will text you my address," she said and kissed my lips as she walked away.

"Damn! This girl is fine! I'm not sure why she decided to give me a chance, but I'm glad she did. I walked out of that warehouse, happy as hell. The next day I had to make some stops and check on my workers. I pulled up on my crew down in North Philly, just as Cam pulled up behind me.

"What's up, bro?" I dapped him up.

"What's up man? You heard Steve and Zeno had a problem out West with one of Jax's men? I thought that nigga retired, and he still moving weed and shit out there," Cam stated.

"Yeah, I heard, I plan on paying his bitch ass a visit. Either he gone stop selling, or his lil' funky ass ten percent is done!" I told him.

"That's what the fuck I'm talking about, I wouldn't have paid his ass shit," Cam said, and I laughed.

"You sound like Law; he didn't want to pay him the percentage as well. You know Law still in his bag about his pops, and how he did us over that Tron issue years ago," I replied.

"Heyyyyyy Sin," this chick named Bird sang out as they walked in the store.

"What's up!" I spoke.

"Bird got one big ass on her, damn! Too bad she a fucking hoe, I heard her ass was fucking with Tone out in South Philly. Now she all on your dick, these chicks be on one," Cam stated.

"They trying to get that bag, like the rest of us," I shrugged.

"Yoooo, I saw Love and all I can say is Gooodddd Damn! Has Law seen her yet?" Cam questioned.

"Yep, and that shit almost drove my nigga crazy!" I laughed.

"The way she's looking, that shit would have driven my ass crazy too," Cam joked.

"Let me get out of here, I have a date with Tee tonight," I smiled.

"Nigga, she finally gave your ass a chance?" he asked.

"I guess you can say that," I responded, and dapped him up to leave. I told him to make sure he checks on the corner boys and let me know what was up. By the time I made it home, it was time for me to get dressed, so I could pull up on Tee. I think I did good in buying this house, it's not too big and flashy. It's a five-bedroom, five-bathroom beautiful home with all of the amenities.

Now I need to fill it up with my very own family. Every time I thought about my own family, I knew it was time for me to settle down. I wasn't getting any younger. I decided on a pair of Givenchy jeans and t-shirt and jumped in the shower. It was going on seven when I arrived at Tee's house, and this shit was crazy big! Damn, baby girl was gettin' that fucking paper. She gave me the code to get in the gate, she said the code would change at 7:15 so I wanted to make sure I was on time. I got out of the car and walked up and rang the doorbell. A few minutes later the door opened, and a green plastic gun was pointed at my leg.

"Who you, lil' nigga?" the kid asked, and I turned around to see if I was being punk'd.

"Yeahhh, state your business, son," a little girl with missing teeth spoke up, and I burst into laughter. These lil' niggas were 'bout it, and I hate to beat somebody's kids' ass. But I will fuck a kid up, these hands don't give a damn who they touch.

"Can you go and get Tee for me?" I asked them.

"We will if you give us fifty dollars," the little girls said, and held her hand out.

"What?! I'm not giving yo' little snagga tooth ass fifty dollars!" I yelled.

"I guess you won't be getting none of my aunt Tee tonight, nigga!" the boy yelled and slammed the door.

"What the fuck just happened?" I spoke out loud. I pulled out my phone and dialed Tee's number, and I got no answer. I rang the doorbell again, and these two lil' badass kids were back.

"Fifty a piece, and you can come in," Snagga said. I pulled out my damn money and counted off a hundred dollars and gave it to their badasses.

"Oh yeah, one more thing! If you get my auntie pregnant

you better be a man about it, or I'm coming for you," Lil' Tyga said. That's exactly who this lil' punk ass devil looked like, the rapper Tyga.

"Auntie! Your little date is here," Snagga pushed the button on the wall. I can't believe I just got robbed for a hundred fucking dollars. I'm about to push one of these lil' damn Bae-Bae kids.

"Sin, I see you made it!" Tee came walking down the stairs, with some chick following behind her.

"Yeah, I met your niece and nephew. You got an interesting set of kids running around here, they sure know how to hustle to get what they want," I laughed.

"Oh shit! What did they do to you? Sin, I'm sorry, this is my sister Journey and the kids belong to her," Tee stated, with a smile.

"Oh good, so they don't live here?" I asked, and they burst out laughing.

"No, they don't live here. I know my kids bad as hell, but they are so loveable," Journey stated, and I looked at her ass like she was crazy!

"Keylin and Kamira, come on your mother is ready to go!" Tee yelled out.

"Mommy, can we go to the store on our way home?" Snagga asked her mother and smiled at me.

"Yes, y'all tell Mr. Sin and Aunt Tee, goodnight," Journey told them.

"Goodnight Mr. Sin, it was nice meeting you," Snagga sang out, and I wanted to make her bottom teeth match her top.

The lil' heifer was so nice now, compared to when she snuffed me for my damn bread!

"It was nice meeting you, Mr. Sin," Tyga said, and this lil' nigga lost the damn bandana that was wrapped around his head and now he had a damn bow tie clipped on the dress shirt he was wearing. These lil' niggas was some lil' ass con artists. I could only burst into laughter; the shit was so damn funny.

"What's so funny?" Tee asked.

"Man, these kids are a mess and I can tell they're related to you," I told Tee. She smiled as she walked her sister and her kids to the door. When she returned, she invited me into her family room.

"Would you like something to drink?" she asked me.

"Sure, just pour me up something nice," I replied.

"Are you ready to eat dinner, or do you want to relax for a minute?" she questioned as she handed me the drink.

"Let's just talk for a minute. So, tell Ms. Tee what caused you to get in the game?" I looked over at her.

"The same reasons it caused you to get in the game. Money has always been my motivation, being able to take care of my family. Growing up it has always been me and Journey! Our mother was too busy running behind her man to even give a damn. One day Journey and I came home from school and she was gone.

"She packed all her shit and left our ass right there in the projects. I had to get it how we lived, in order to feed my little sister. I was only sixteen and Journey was fourteen. We followed our routine every day as if my mom lived there. We made a vow to never tell anyone that she left us. I knew the state would put us in foster care, and I never wanted Journey separated from me. Our neighbor Ms. Carrie found out that my mom had left, so she looked out for us until I turned eighteen. Let's just say Ms. Carrie is living the good life these days. I could never repay her for what she has done for us," Tee stated, and I now understood why she went so hard.

"I feel you lil' mama, and I respect that shit. I like the way you move, but the game is getting uglier by the day. So, I need you to be careful out there in those streets," I said to her.

"I got me and you in these streets. Don't you worry about a thing," Tee stated.

"Oh yeah, how you got me?" I was interested in her statement she had just made.

"You've been moving this dope all crazy like, I mean your crew has been selling about five mil in three to four weeks tops. That's a lot of weight," she spoke.

"Nah, that's us just testing the waters. You ain't seen movement like we're getting ready to move. I plan on stepping out on the west coast, we already set up shop and I need you to supply me out there as well. I know you just took over the west coast, and I trust you," I told her.

"Oh, you've been doing your homework, we can talk about it over dinner," she smiled. I leaned over and kissed her lips, I slipped my tongue in her mouth. She began sucking that muthafucka like she was starving.

"Or we can discuss it after you fuck the shit out of me,"

she moaned out, and I lifted her ass, and placed her on her back.

"Why are you playing with me lil' mama? You've been playing with me for years knowing I wanted your ass," I gritted as I nibbled on her bottom lip.

"I've been taking my time getting to know you, it's hard to trust someone in this game. So, allowing you into my life, my home, and my bed was calculated and thought out. One more thing, once you enter my sacred place, this Meka bitch is a done deal!" Teana stated as she began sucking on my neck.

"Who the fuck is Meka?" I laughed, and she smiled up at me.

"That's what I like to hear," she purred, and I damn near tore her clothes off. I slid my finger up and down her center, as she moaned out my name. That shit damn near drove me crazy, as she gyrated on my fingers and her fluids leaked out of her.

"Damn you wet!" I gritted, as I kissed down her body sucking and licking on her nipples.

"Who wet?! Sincere Devonte Williams, I know damn well you didn't call me and you over there fucking! She better be a good wholesome Christian, and you better put a raincoat on that lil' ass dick of yours. That heifer better not be a hoe, or crazy!" my mother's voice came blaring through the speaker. I must have accidentally dialed her ass. *What the fuck?* I grabbed the phone and hung up on her ass.

"Let your mother know, I'm not a hoe, but I can get crazy

at any given time," Tee moaned out, as she continued to gyrate on my fingers.

"She crazy as hell too, I think you two will get along just fine," I whispered.

"Shit! I need you to fuck me and don't play with me, Sin!" she spoke, and I didn't plan on playing with her at all. I was getting ready to fuck her life all the way up. I grabbed a condom from my wallet and pulled my boxers off. When my dick came into view, her eyes damn near popped out of her sockets. She quickly recovered, and I guess she anticipated the ride. I slid the condom on and hovered over her.

"The only thing I want to play with is your insides, baby," I whispered as I slid in her with force.

"Fuckkkkk!" she screamed as I continued to wreak havoc on her pussy. I must say she caught me off guard because she had some good pussy.

"Oh fuck!" I gritted, as I bit down on my lips trying to hold in the growl that I wanted to let out. As I continued to pump in and out of her, we went at it for damn near two hours fucking in every position possible. I flipped her over and began hitting it from the back.

"Ohhhhh shit, I..... Shhhhhhhhhit! Fuck me!"

"Come on lil' mama, throw that ass back on this muthafucka!" I growled, and baby girl went to work on my dick.

"Ohhhhh shit! Fuccckkkkkkkkk!" I roared, as I felt the force of her cumming. She damn near pushes my dick out of her. Her screams sent me over the edge as I released in my condom.

"So, what are we doing? Are we exclusive or we just fuck-ing?" I asked her as I kissed her lips.

"Right now, we are getting to know each other. I'm not sure if I'm ready for a relationship, let's just take it slow," she stated, and I was cool with what she wanted.

Chapter Ten

LOVE

I was kicking my damn self for not telling Law about Savion. Everyone was down my throat about it and my cousin Tay was not helping at all.

"Cuz let's get out the house and go down south street to do some shopping, and maybe a lil' drink or two. It's been a minute since we have been down there, let's go have some fun. I'm tired of sitting in the house with these old people," Tay stated, and I had to agree with her. We have been handling business and getting prepared for my mother's funeral tomorrow. It's been so bad that I haven't even taken my son out of the house. I'm grateful that he had his little cousins to play with.

"Okay, let's go," agreeing with her. By the time we got dressed, it was almost eight. My grandmother agreed to watch Savi for me, while we hung out for a little bit. When we made it down to South Street, we grabbed a drink from Fat Tuesdays and walked the strip.

"Look at that, it's a tattoo shop let's go in there and get a tattoo," Tay suggested.

"Girl, I'm not getting a tattoo, besides there is only one person that I would ever let tattoo me," I told her.

"Ohhh you mean, the person that gave you that fucking Bentley, and all that damn money in the five damn purses you got? By the way thanks for the clothes, I was glad your ass couldn't fit them. Now I can stunt on these hoes," Tay laughed, this girl was crazy. We walked into the tattoo shop, and I was blown away. This damn place had a bar and served food on one side of it. It was big as hell in here and very nice.

"Dayum! This place is the fuck LIT!" Tay yelled out.

"Hello, Welcome to Ink Drip, are you ladies here for dinner and drinks? Or do you have a tattoo appointment?" the lady asked.

"I wanted to get a tattoo, is that possible?" Tay asked her.

"If you don't have an appointment, the shop does not have any openings until March," she told Tay, and I think we were both confused.

"Ma'am, that's seven months away," I said to her.

"Yes Ma'am, I know. Mr. Williams and all of his artists come highly requested and that's his schedule right now. In order to get in with him, you would have to book at least six months ahead," she replied.

"Damn, what the hell he drippin' on people, Platinum?!" Tay shouted, and I laughed at her ass.

"Love," someone called out from behind us. I turned, and it was Law. What are the odds of me running into him?

"Law, hello," I spoke.

"What are you doing down here?" he asked.

"I wanted to get a tattoo, but it seems that these niggas drip platinum and gold on you! So, the waiting list is hella long. I guess we will have to go down the street where the regular people go," Tay said to him.

"What were you trying to get? I could ink you real quick," he told her.

"I want a big butterfly on my back, with baby butterflies flying around," she responded.

"This might be a two-visit job, but I got you. Love, what about you?" he questioned, as he looked at me.

"Oh nooo, I'm not getting anything done. You work here?" I asked him, and he smiled.

"As a matter of fact, I do, I own the place," he stated, and my mouth was agape.

"Oh my god! You did it, you really did it, Savion!" I hugged him, without thinking. He wrapped his arms around me, and someone was clearing their throat.

"Hello," a beautiful girl walked up to us.

"Hey, babe! Love, Tay, this is my beautiful fiancé, Shantel. Shantel, this is Love, and her cousin Tay," he introduced and kissed her on the lips.

"Love, it's nice to finally put a face with the name. I've heard a lot about you, none of it was good," this bitch said.

"Shantel, what the fuck?! Why you out here starting shit?!" Law angrily questioned her.

"Oh, this bitch tried it! Bitch, I will beat you the fuck up in here. Come for my cousin again and let me show you this North Philly beat down! Love let's go before I beat this bitch up off GP! She looks like she can't fight so that shit won't even be fair, stank pussy ass hoe!" Tay went off on this Shantel bitch.

"Bitch, you don't know me or what I'm capable...." Shantel was speaking and was cut off when Tay punched the shit out of her.

"Capable that, hoe!" Tay yelled.

"Shantel, is it? Don't speak on shit you don't know about!" I told her, and we left. I could hear Law and her arguing as we headed out.

"Girl, I was about to beat that bitch ugly, you hear me! That punch wasn't shit, she gone catch this fade before it's all said and done! Urggggggghhhh, I hate snooty bitches like her!" Tay fussed, as we walked back to the car. I see Law had a lot to say about me to his girl. The shocking part about all of this is that he's getting married; wow times have really changed.

Chapter Eleven

LAW

I felt bad about what Shantel said to Love, but there wasn't much I could do about it. I will apologize to her when I see her today at the funeral. I was on my way to the church and I was running late. Sin and my mom both had texted me and said the family was already inside the church. I parked and hopped out of the car, by the time I got in the church the family was at the casket. Love was a complete mess, and my heart ached for her. There was a little boy standing and holding her hand. Tay walked up and pulled him away with her and they took a seat. I found my mom, and Sin thank god they saved me a seat because the church was packed.

"Who is the kid with Love?" I asked them.

"I don't know he walked in with her," Sin stated.

"Something looked familiar about the little boy, I couldn't really get a good look at him," my mother whispered.

"Damn, I got to use the bathroom, I will be right back," I told them. I was standing at the sink washing my hands, and I could hear talking at the door.

"Hurry up, Savi and use the bathroom. Don't forget to wash your hands," I heard a woman say, and a little boy walked in. He seemed to be struggling to reach the urinal.

"You need some help lil' man?" I asked him.

"I do, but don't tell my mommy. I'm a big boy," he stated. I walked over and lifted him up as he handled his business.

"Your secret is safe with me," I whispered to him. He finished up and washed his hands, I handed him a paper towel.

"Alright, lil' homie," I held my hand out to shake his. It was something about this kid, that held my attention.

"My name is Savion Jaxon Williams, Jr. not homie, What's your name?" he questioned, but I was still stuck, on his fucking name.

"My name is Savion Jaxon Williams," I told him, as the fire started to rise from the pit of my damn stomach.

"That's cool, we have the same name you don't have a Jr. But that's okay, we have the same rest of the name," he happily spoke.

"What is your mother's name?" I asked him.

"My mommy's name is Love Chandler Hill, but she hates the Hill part," he stated, and I turned and walked out the door and was met with a surprised look on Tay's face. I stormed back inside the church, with Tay and the little boy behind me.

"Law, please wait until the funeral is over, please," I heard Tay calling out for me. But it was too late I was already moving to the front of the church. I heard Tay yell out to Love, and the church was in an uproar.

"Lovvvvveeee bitch, runnnnnnn!" Tay screamed, and Love stood and turned to see me coming.

"Is that my fucking, son!" I roared in her face! I could see my mother and brother approaching but this was not the fucking time.

"Law, this is my mother's funeral. Can we please discuss this later?" she whispered with a very nervous look on her face.

"We will do this shit, right now!" I gritted, as I grabbed her arm and pulled her closer to me.

"Get off my mommy!" Savion yelled as he kicked me. I let her go, and I remained in her face waiting for her to answer me.

"Answer me, dammit!" I roared.

"Son, come on let's go, we will get the answers we need later!" my mom urged as she pulled on my arm.

"You got one second to answer me, or I'm dragging your ass out of here! Is he my son, Love?" she turned and looked at her grandmother and Ms. Josephine was clearly upset. When she turned back to face me, her face was full of tears. I didn't even need her to answer, at that very moment I knew what her answer would be. Tay and some of her other cousins had taken Savion out of the church.

"Yes, he is your son! I'm so sorry," she cried.

"Oh, dear lord!" I heard my mother cry out.

"Sorry! Bitch, you are fucking selfish! Do you understand what the fuck you have done! Urrggggggggghhhhhhhhh!" I wanted to knock this girl the fuck out. But the man in me wouldn't allow me to do that.

"Bruh, come on let's go outside," Sin spoke, and I could only turn and walk away. Yet again, this girl has hurt me to the fucking core! Why the fuck would she do that shit, why would she fucking deny me of my fucking kid! I was ready to tear this church the fuck up, but I have disrespected Ms. Evelyn's funeral and I will apologize to Ms. Josephine later. When we walked out of the church, lil' man was with Tay clearly upset.

"Son, you have to give him a minute. All he saw you do was yell and scream at his mother. I don't think he is going to be happy to see you right now," my mom spoke.

"How is it, that I come out looking like the bad person, when his selfish ass mother is the one that keeps stomping on my damn heart! When the fuck will I matter, mom!" I roared. I was angry as hell, and Love fucking Hill was going to have to deal with this fucking volcano that was going to erupt all over her ass!

Chapter Twelve

SIN

This shit is crazy as fuck! I can't believe that Love did this shit!

"Sin stay out here with your brother. I'm going in the church for the rest of the funeral. This is a damn mess, but that is still that girl's mother and she is hurting right now. We have to give her that respect," my mom said.

"Respect! Are you serious right now, mom? The bitch didn't give me any respect, she took my fucking kid. I missed everything! She let another nigga go through the most important times in his life, and just said fuck me. So, nah, she gets no respect from me!" Law yelled, and my mom smacked the shit out of him.

"Let me tell you something! I raised you better than that, you will have respect for this girl's mother and Ms. Josephine. Allow them to bury their loved one, and then you handle this shit with Love. Remember Love doesn't live here anymore, and she can snatch him up and get the fuck out of town on your ass," Mom said to him.

"That shit is dead! She won't be taking my child nowhere, not until he is tested, and I know for sure that he's mine," Law told her. My mom turned and went back inside the church shaking her head. Law walked over to where Tay and the little boy was sitting. I decided to follow him, so I could actually meet the kid.

"Savion, can we talk?" Law asked him.

"I guess," Savion shrugged.

"I'm sorry, I didn't mean to yell at your mother," Law said to him.

"I know who you are, you look different now," Savion responded.

"Oh yeah, how do you know who I am?" Law questioned.

"Because of this!" he said, pulling a chain with a Bible locket charm from under his shirt. Law opened it, and I damn near shed a tear. It was a picture of Law when he was younger, and on the other side, it read. '*My dad is the best dad in the world!*'

"That's a nice locket you have, how old are you, Savion?" Law asked him, as he wiped the tears from his eyes.

"I'm going to be six soon," Savion replied.

"That's great, you're a big boy," Law smiled at him.

"Mommy and I pray for you every night, and we always say we love you too! But you were mean to mommy, and I'm mad at you," Lil' man, said and he damn sure was his father's child.

Because it takes a long damn time for Law to come down when he's pissed.

"Savi, there is your mother, we have to go," he grabbed Tay's hand and walked off with her. But he stopped, and ran back to Law, and wrapped his little arms around his legs.

"I love you, dad," he said and ran back over to Tay. Damn! That shit broke both of our asses down.

"Man, how could she do that shit to me?" Law looked at me, with his red eyes.

"I don't have an answer for you, bro. But what I do know, is that your son is watching everything you do concerning him, and his mother. You have to move carefully when you're dealing with them. I know what she did is fucked up, you are gonna have to figure this shit out baby bro," I said to him, as we watched the family get in the funeral cars. My phone was beeping which let me know I had a text.

Teana: I enjoyed you last night.

Me: You can enjoy me every night, just as long as you keep Snagga and Tyga away from me.

Teana: Are you going to ever tell me what they did to you?

Me: Let's just say they got the drop on me!

Teana: Lol. I watched the security footage. I can't believe you let a six and eight-year-old take you for yo' paper.

Me: We need to put they asses on the payroll.

Teana: Nah, they need to be on the straight and narrow.

Me: Girl bye, they gone be in the trap by the time they lil' hustlin' asses turn ten. You saw the way they handled my ass. With a water gun at that!

Teana: Lol. I will see you later tonight. I slipped my phone back in my pocket and went to join my brother and mother.

"So, what's the plan?" I asked them.

"I'm going to my apartment; I need to clear my head. I won't be able to do that at my house with Shantel breathing down my neck," Law stated.

"You know you are going to have to let her know what's going on, son," Mom said to him.

"I know, I will talk to y'all later," he said, and walked off. I kissed my mom and jumped in my car to go check on my new club I'm opening this weekend. I'm praying my brother can work this shit out and get a real chance at knowing his son.

Chapter Thirteen

LOVE

*M*y heart was breaking; the look in his eyes broke every part of me. I didn't want him to find out this way. I knew it would be risky having my son at the funeral, but I never imagined that Law would go off like that. I was so embarrassed that it all happened in front of everyone and now that's all my family could talk about. We had made it back to the house, and my grandmother decided to only have close family come over. I was so thankful for that; I just didn't want to see anyone right now. Tay walked into the room with a plate in her hand.

"Here boo, you have to eat something," Tay said as she handed me the plate.

"I'm really not hungry, I'm just so mad at myself for making such a dumb decision. I was mad at him, I thought he was still in the drug game and I didn't want Savi around it.

Nor did I want to put my son in danger. I know it's no excuse, but that was all I could think about. The night at my party, that shooting scared the shit out of me. I was afraid for him, I thought I would lose him to the streets," I cried.

"It's going to be alright, L. You just have to give him some time and he is going through it right now," Tay said as my phone went off. It was a text from Ms. Naomi.

Naomi: Love, he wants to see you. He is at his apartment 1901 Presidential Blvd. right off of City Ave.

Me: Okay, thanks.

"What?" Tay questioned.

"He wants to see me," I looked over at her.

"Oh, hell nawl! Girl, you better not take your ass over there. That nigga is going to kill you and stuff your ass in the dumpster. Can I have your car? Because you not coming back for it! Fuck that, I would sit my happy ass right here in the comforts of my grandmother's house. Where all the knives and Josephine's shotgun is," Tay said getting all damn hype.

"Tay, I need to talk to him, I will be fine. He is angry but he won't hurt me," I told her.

"Make sure you leave that address with me, and yo' ass better text me when you get there, and about thirty minutes after you get in the house. That nigga can't be trusted right now, and if his fine ass brother there call me so I can come over," Tay said, as she gyrated around the room.

"Girl, I'm sure he has a girlfriend," I told her, as I stood to leave.

"I can change his mind and sway his ass Tay's way," she

said, and I could only laugh at her. By the time I made it to the address, it was a little after nine. I took a deep breath and stepped out of the car. I walked in and the security guard was sitting at the desk.

"Good evening ma'am. How can I help you?" he asked.

"Hi, I'm here to see Savion Williams," I replied with a smile. I was nervous as hell because I knew he was beyond pissed. The guard picked up the phone and dialed a number.

"Mr. Williams, you have someone here to see you," he advised.

"Ma'am take the elevators to P20 and It will take you directly into his penthouse," the guard directed me. I got on the elevator and waited for the doors to open. When the bell sounded the doors opened and he was standing there. We stared at each other for a few minutes, until I looked away.

"I need you to start talking. Tell me why, why you would do some shit like that to me?" he asked me.

"I'm so sorry, I never wanted to hurt you. I didn't want him to be involved in the street life. I never wanted our son to get hurt, by the decisions you made. I was only thinking of him and his well-being," I cried.

"No, you were only thinking of yourself! You never gave me an option to make the right decision concerning him. You never thought about me or him, he missed six years without having me! I missed every important moment, his first steps, and his first words! I can't get that shit back," he angrily spat. I walked up to him and touched his arm and he snatched away from me.

"Don't fucking touch me, I wanted you to talk not touch me!" he roared.

"Law, I'm sorry, I don't know what else to say," I cried, as I tried to touch him again. He grabbed me and pinned me up against the wall. He was so close to me that our nose's touched.

"I want a test! If he is indeed mine, you better find a job here in Philly! Because I be damn if he is going back to Miami. You let that pussy ass nigga raise my fucking son!" he yelled, and my phone vibrated. It was Tay calling, so I grabbed it.

"Hello," I answered.

"Bitch, you alright? You could have sent a smoke signal a fucking hooty-hoo or something, damn! I done smoked all of grandma fucking weed, waiting on you to call. She gone be mad as hell when she goes in her stash and that shit gone!" she spoke.

"I'm fine, I will be there soon," I told her and ended the call.

"Listen, Savion, I know you are angry. But I'm not leaving Miami, I have a life there and Savi loves it there. I can't just change our lives because you say so, I will be more than happy to work out an agreement with you. However, me moving back is not up for debate!" I stood my ground, and that was it for me.

"We will see about that, see yourself out and I want to spend time with my son!" he stated.

"Don't you want to get tested first, to make sure he is

yours?" I said to him. At this point I no longer gave a damn. He hit below the belt with that one, and I was done with his disrespect.

"Don't fucking push me! Right now, I'm unstable and all I want to do is wring your fucking neck! So, don't fuck with me, Love," he gritted, I could feel the heat off of his breath. I knew I shouldn't be thinking about this, but I loved this man. I loved him with everything in me, and it has been damn three years since I had sex.

"Law, I love you," I whispered.

"Get the fuck out!" he roared glaring down at me. He turned and walked away, I got on the elevator and left. My heartfelt like it was going to burst, I hated that we were in this situation. I hated that I held on to this love for him, for so long and did nothing about it. He hated me, and there was nothing I could do about it. By the time I made it back to my grandmother's house they were having a good time. Drinking, eating, and playing cards.

"Thank god! Girl I'm so glad to see yo' ass. I just knew you were a goner; I had picked your dress out for you and every-thing," Tay laughed.

"What dress, what are you talking about?" I asked her.

"The dress for your funeral," she said, and this girl had a dress laid out on the bed.

"You was gone be one sharp dead heifer, that's for sure!" We both burst out laughing.

"Girl stop it! He is so hurt, Tay. I told him I loved him, and he put me out," I said to her.

"Bitch! I would have put yo' confused ass out too. How you gone go in that man shit, talking 'bout you love him, and you done hid a whole baby away from his ass! Damn that dick must have had gold dripping from that shit!" She laughed, as I looked over at Savi sleeping. I couldn't help but to feel bad, his dad was right. I did cheat them both from getting to know each other.

"Taymar, where the hell is my damn weed!" my grandma yelled.

"Grammy, how am I supposed to know? Your high ass probably smoked it! You have been throwing them back grandma, maybe you don't remember smoking it. I stopped smoking remember?" Tay dumb ass said to her.

"Yeah, you might be right, I think I did smoke it," my Grammy said, Tay and I fell out laughing.

"Love, did you work things out with Law? I have never seen him so angry before, but I told you this would blow up in your face. Y'all can't be playing with these men and think there will be no repercussions later on," my grandmother stated.

"We spoke, but nothing has been resolved. I hope he will come around and want to work things out with me. I think he is going to give me a hard time about going back to Miami," I spoke.

"Miami! Bitch, you better gone down to CVS, Rite Aid, or Walgreens and see if them niggas hiring. You gone be one pill poppin hoe right here in Philly! We might as well go celebrate tomorrow. There is a new club opening up, and I'm trying to drop it low for a bunch of real niggas!" Tay said, and grandma just shook her head.

"Taymar, take your ass to bed somewhere!" Grammy told her.

"Grammy, it's still early we about to go outside and chill for a little while," Tay told her, and I was down with that. It was a little after eleven, so to us, the night was still young. I hope tomorrow is a better day.

Chapter Fourteen

LAW

an, I was on fucking fire! The nerve of this girl, the shit she was spittin' was bullshit. I decided to come home and talk to Shantel about what happened today.

"Babe, what's wrong?" she asked as she sat in my lap.

"I found out that Love has a son, and I'm his father," I spoke.

"What?! How do you know he's your son?" she asked.

"We are getting tested, but I can look at him and tell that he's my child," I responded.

"Oh my god, she didn't even say shit to you. What a fucking bitch! That's the type of bitch you call a friend. She kept your so-called child away from you all these years!" Shantel yelled.

"Please don't say that again, I think I've done enough of

disrespecting her today. Don't disrespect her, if he's my son I will never allow his mother to be disrespected. I will never allow you to be disrespected," I stated.

"Fuck that, she doesn't deserve respect and how can you stand in my face and defend her after what she has done? We need to go and get him right now, she doesn't deserve to have him," she fussed.

"Shantel, I would never take him from his mother. I do believe she will go to war over her child, and so would I. He is fine where he is, but I do plan on spending time with him. I don't know him, so that means she will be with him until I get to know him," I told her.

"Like hell she will, you are not spending time with that B....," she caught herself.

"This is the way it will be, until I get to know him," I pulled her into me, and crashed my lips into her. The urgency of me being inside of her was about to kill me. I needed to release some of this fucking anger. I flipped her over and pulled my sweats down and pushed my dick in her so damn fast. She screamed out as I dug deep into her pussy.

"Fuck! What has gotten into you? Oh shit, yessss fuck me daddy!" she screamed, I felt like I was going to break my dick off in her ass. The deeper I went in her, the harder I became, and the more Loves face appeared. I continued to thrust in and out of her, as she screamed louder, gripping the sheets.

"I'm cumming babe, fuck I'm cumming!" she moaned.

"Fuckkkkkkkkk!" I roared as I released inside of her.

"Damn, what was that all about? You have never fucked

me like that. I have to say I liked it; we need to do that more often," Shantel said, as I stood to go take a shower without saying a word. I have to get over this shit, Love has never entered my mind while making love to Shantel. This can't be happening now, what the fuck!

The next day, I had to make a few runs before getting ready for the grand opening of LUX. Sin was excited about his new club, and I was happy for him. A few hours later I pulled up to the valet, stepping out of my car and walking inside the club. DaBaby- *Suge* was blasting through the speakers, it was definitely packed up in here. I walked up to VIP, Sin had this shit LIT.

"Ahhhhh shit, Law, is in the muthafuckin' building, ladies back up off my nigga! I know yo' panties are wet, but my dude is officially off the market! Congrats, bro!" the DJ yelled out and I threw up my hand.

"Bruh, you made it, this shit is straight fya tonight!" Sin spoke over the music.

"Yeah, I'm happy for you man, you did your thing with this right here!" I told him.

"Damn, look who just walked in! Got damnnnn! Is that fucking Tay? Damn she fine as hell, I ain't never seen her ass looking like that," Sin stated, as I looked at Love. This girl was off the charts fine, and there wasn't shit I could do about it. I was faithful and loyal to my girl; I couldn't wait to marry her ass in a couple of weeks.

"I'm about to invite them up," Sin said, and I shrugged. I didn't really care what he did. I took a seat and poured me a drink, just as I began to vibe to the music. Love and Tay walked into VIP and every nigga up in this shit was drooling. Love had on a bodycon dress that fit every fucking curve she had and damn she had plenty. Tay had on a pair of jeans with a crop top. Sin was right, she was definitely killin' it tonight.

"What's up, Law?" Tay spoke as they took a seat on the couch next to me.

"What's good," I spoke. Love decided not to speak, and I was cool with that.

"Tay, I didn't know your ass was this fine," Sin told her, and I shook my damn head.

"That's what they tell me, but don't you have a girl?" she questioned.

"I have a friend, but nothing is official with us. Unless you trying to make it official," Sin stated.

"Nigga, I'm not with the bullshit! I come with all the shits; I tell you exactly what I want so we don't have to play the guessing game. Like right now, I'm going to sip on these drinks, put one or two in the air and ride yo' dick until the sun comes up!" Tay said to him, and a smile crept across his lips as he got himself together.

"Well damn, my lil' nigga ready whenever you are!" Sin responded. Tay poured two drinks, and she handed one to Love.

"So, you just not gone speak to my cousin?" Tay asked me.

"Nahh, she good! She don't need me to speak to her," I replied.

"Damn, it's like that? You need to get over this shit, and work things out with her. Y'all have a son to raise," Tay spoke.

"Please, tell me when was she worried about us raising our son? Was she worried when she found out she was pregnant, was she worried when she felt him kick, was she worried when she gave birth, was she fucking worried on his first birthday, the second, or the fucking fourth birthday! Tell me Tay, when the fuck was she exactly worried?" I roared.

"Mmmmm mmmmm, nope, hell Nawl! Ion even think that bitch was worried at all!" Tay stated.

"Tay!" Love yelled.

"Girl what? That nigga look like he bout to foam at the mouth. The best thing for us to do is agree with his ass. Black hoes matter! Fight the muthafuckin power," she said, and I just shook my head.

"I'm going downstairs," Love told her, as she stood and walked off. At this point, I don't give a fuck how shit comes out! I'm so fucking mad, I felt as if I was going to fucking explode!

Fucking with Tay was going to get my ass in a world of trouble, but the way she was riding this dick. She had my fucking toes throwing up gang signs, and my damn eyes were rolling in the back of my damn head.

"Fuck this pussy wet!" I gritted as she bit down on her bottom lip, grinding on my dick.

"Nigga, ohhhhh shit this dick is gooood! Ahhhhhhh fuck, the lawwd blessed yo' ass!" She screamed as she took this dick. Damn, I didn't know lil' mama had it like that. I think this is the best pussy I ever had, I thought Tee shit was good. But damn! Ms. Tay got my ass ready to marry her and this chick just slid on the pipe an hour ago!

I'm glad me and Tee didn't solidify what we had going on yet. Right now, we were just fucking, I need to call my damn mama and talk about this shit. I flipped her over doggy style and fucked the dog shit out of her ass. The way she was grip-ping my dick had a nigga ready to shed a fucking tear! Nah this good pussy bitch gotta go! I tried to pull out of her, and the pussy sucked my shit back in, right before my fucking eyes. I pulled out of her ass so quick, fuck that! Ion even want to fuck that type of pussy, that shit is like a fucking drug. She ain't gone have my ass running around here feenin' for my next hit! Fuck that!

"What's wrong?" she asked as she began rubbing her pussy. This girl was a damn freak and I was fucking scared. Fuck that my mama and I gotta talk to-fucking-night.

"Ummmm I gotta go, I just remembered I had to go check on my mama," I stuttered, as she moaned out grinding on her fingers. This shit was fucking amazing to watch.

"Come on baby, just make me cum, that's all I want you to do," she moaned, and my ole turncoat ass dick jumped. This nigga needed to pick a team, and I see his ass wanted to be on team muthafuckin' Tay! Fuck it, I sent up a prayer that I would be the same man after I was done. I slid back in her, and I swear the pussy was so good a nigga had tears flowing. You might as well say, she was fucking me. Because my ole soft ass was fucking stuck! I ain't never in my life had no pussy like this.

"Damn Zaddy, I'm cumming! Ohhhhhh fuck!" she screamed, as we both came together. I was officially in fucking love! Come on let's get cleaned up so I can take you home. About an hour later, I pulled up in front of Ms. Josephine's house. She put her hand on the latch to open the door and I pulled her into me. I tried to suck her damn face off, just thinking about her pussy gave my ass the jitters.

"Let me take you to dinner tonight?" I asked her since it was damn near six in the morning.

"That would be nice, just call me," she said and got out the car. Once she was in the house, I pulled off heading straight to my mom's crib. I knew my mom was sleep but her ass had to wake the fuck up. We needed to talk about this shit, and she had to help me figure this all out.

"Mom!" I yelled out. I knew she would come downstairs going off. I didn't care I was ready to get cursed out.

"Nigga! I know yo' black ass ain't in my house, this early in the morning screaming and shit! What the fuck is wrong with you?!" she yelled.

"Ma, I fucked this girl, and oh my GOD!" I stated as I paced back and forth.

"What?! She burned you, her pussy was stank?! Nigga spit it out! I told you and yo' brother about fucking these dirty ass hoes out here. Now look at you, yo' damn dick bout to fall the fuck off! Let me put some clothes on so we can go get yo' shit checked out," she went on and on.

"No ma, I fucked her, and the pussy was soooooo fucking good! The shit was so good, I cried! I'm ready to marry her ass today!" I told her.

"Nigga, you woke me up because you done got pussy whipped. Who the fuck did that shit to you?" she questioned.

"Love cousin, Tay," I said to her.

"Oh lawwwwd, why y'all niggas fucking with girls I'm fond

of! I already got to kick Loves ass, for keeping my damn grandson away from me. Your brother over there ready to commit murder, and now you want to go over there fucking with Josephine other granddaughter. Y'all niggas gone drive me crazy!" she fussed and went upstairs.

"Ma! Where are you going? We need to figure this shit out together!" I yelled out. She came back down the stairs and shook her head.

"What the fuck you want me to do? I can't help that the girl got good pussy. You thought you were gone be out here slinging dick, and not get caught up! Well the girl done pussy whipped you, and that's the end of that," she frowned and went back upstairs. My mom was no damn help, I decided to go get in my bed and sleep the day away.

Chapter Sixteen

LOVE

I knew Law would be angry with me, but his ass was being so damn disrespectful towards me. He was actually going overboard with the shit, and it was pissing me off. I was due to go back to Miami in the morning, I needed to handle some business with my job. I was planning to take a leave of absence so that I could come back and let Savi spend time with his father.

"Mommy, is my dad still mad at us?" Savi asked.

"No baby, why would you say that?" I questioned.

"Because he was mad," he pouted, as he rested his chin in the palm of his hand.

"Savi, he was never mad at you. There are some things that your dad and I have to work through. But he could never be mad at you," I told him and pulled him in for a hug. I have always talked to Savi about his father. Shown him pictures of his dad, but they were all from back in the day. I didn't have anything current of him, Savi must have figured it out. He is a smart kid and will be turning five in less than a week. I heard a knock at the door, and Tay walked into the room.

"Savi, your grandmother has lunch ready for you," Tay told him.

"What time did you get in last night?" I smiled at her.

"You mean this morning, girl that nigga was acting all kinds of weird. I think I popped this pussy power on his ass too hard or something. His ass didn't even want to finish! But on God, son, that nigga is all things fucking fine! His damn body is just perfect, and the dick, oh bitch the dick is serious. He is taking me out to dinner tonight," Tay stated, and I was happy for my cousin.

"I'm happy for you boo, I just want you to be careful. Sin is deep in the streets and I want you to really understand what that means," I said to her.

"Girl, I'm from the streets, we were raised in this shit! I'm good, I promise you," she responded.

"Just because we are products of the street, don't mean we have to stay that way," I stated.

"I got this," she replied.

"Love you have guest!" my Grammy called out.

"Oh shit, what if it's Law! Here take this, if that nigga touch you just start slicing. That will give me enough time to get grandma's shotgun," Tay crazy ass said, handing me her switchblade.

"Girl, I don't need that, I can handle whatever Law has for me," I smiled.

"Bitch, not if yo' ass is dead you can't," she stated, looking all crazy.

"Girl, move so I can go see who this is," I told her, and walked out of the room. When I walked in the living room, Law was standing by the door and Ms. Naomi was talking with my grandmother.

"Hello," I greeted them both.

"Hey Love, we wanted to come over and talk to you for a minute," Ms. Naomi spoke.

"I will give you all some time to talk in private," my grandmother said, and left the room.

"Love I'm not going to come down on you about why you felt you had to keep my grandson a secret. I'm sure this boy has given you plenty of hell about that. But I will say this, you can always call me about anything. That child needs to know his family, I don't need a DNA test to know if that's my grandson. He looks just like his father when he was that age, but whatever you and Savion decide on that is fine with me. I just don't think we need to waste any time getting to know my grandbaby. Is it okay, if I meet him?" she asked, and Law was still standing there staring at me.

"I'm sorry that I made this decision. I had so many reasons why I did it, but none of that is an excuse for keeping him away. It's something that I will never be able to forgive myself for. Let me get Savi for you both," I felt the need to apologize to her. None of them deserved what I had done. I just pray that we could all work through this for Savi's sake.

"Savi, you have someone here to see you," I said to him.

"Okay," he stated and got down out of his chair and grabbed my hand. We walked back in the room, and Law instantly moved towards us.

"Hi Savion," he greeted Savi.

"Hi, are you still mad at us?" he asked Law.

"What? No, I could never be mad at you," Law Told him.

"Are you still mad at my mommy?" he asked him.

"Your mom and I will be alright. I want to introduce someone to you. This is your grandmother, Naomi," Law said to him.

"I know," Savi replied, and they both looked over at me.

"Savi has a book that I made for him when he was a baby. He looks in the book every night before he goes to bed. He is a very intelligent little boy; he always has questions and he never forgets anything you tell him. It may have taken him a minute to recognize you all in person, but he knows his grand-mother's name," I spoke, Naomi was in tears at the revelation that he knew who she was.

"Why are you crying? Was he mean to you too?" Savi asked his Grandmother and looked over at Law with a frown on his face.

"No, he wasn't mean to me, your dad is a very nice guy. He's not a mean person, he was just a little upset but he's better now," Naomi looked at him and smiled.

"Okay, do you want to play with my toy?" he walked over

to Law and stood in front of him. Law looked down at him with his red eyes and picked him in for a hug.

"Yes, I would love to play with your toy," he kissed the top of Savi's head, and they played on the floor together.

"Love make sure you bring him over to see me," Ms. Naomi stated.

"Savi and I leave to go back to Miami tomorrow. I do plan on coming back soon, and I will bring him by then," I told her.

"What?! Nahh, that's not gone work for me," Law stood.

"Grandma get yo' gun poppin'! Love 'bout to die!" We heard Tay yell from the back of the house. Her nosey ass must have been in the hall listening to our conversation.

"Law! Watch what you say," Ms. Naomi spoke and looked over at Savi.

"Savi, go in the back with your cousin, Tay," I told him. Once, Savi left the room I looked at Law.

"I know that you want to get to know your son. But I have a life in Miami and business that I need to handle. I was planning to take a leave of absence from my job and then come back to Philly. I can't just stay here without making the proper arrangements," I said to him.

"When do you plan on leaving?" he asked me.

"In the morning, we should be back in a few days," I replied.

"What time is your flight?" he asked, and I was wondering where he was going with this.

"We leave at eight," he just nodded his head.

"I will come and see you both off," he told me.

"Love make sure when you get back to bring him over," Ms. Naomi stood and hugged me. She spoke to her son for a minute and then left. It was just me and Law standing and looking at each other. I hate that this has happened because I really missed talking to him, and I damn sure missed our friendship.

"I would like to say goodbye to him," he said, and I told him to follow me. When I walked into the bedroom, Savi was playing his game.

"Hey lil' man, I'm going to head out and let you and your mom relax. I will see you in the morning, alright," Law said to him.

"You don't want to play with me, you can stay with us if you want too," Savi smiled.

"If it's okay with your mom, I'm cool with it," Law told him. Savi looked over at me and I nodded.

"It's fine, I can go hang with Tay and give you two some-time alone," I said to them.

"Don't bring your ass in my room, I'm going to bed!" Tay yelled out. I just burst into laughter, because my cousin was crazy. I'm sure if I opened the door, her ass would be standing there.

"Tay needs help, but you don't need to leave." Law smiled at me.

I sat down on my bed, as he sat down on the bed next to Savi, and they played with his toys together. I must have fallen asleep, I felt something rub across my cheek. I opened my eyes and Law was standing over me.

"I'm going to head out, lil' man is tired and is sleeping," he whispered, as he stared down at me.

"I'm sorry, I'm a little exhausted with all that has been going on. What time is it?" I questioned.

"It's a little after five, you two have been sleeping for a couple of hours now. I actually just sat here and watched the both of you sleep. We really need to sit down and have a conversation about him," he stated.

"I will call you when I get back, I promise it will only be for a few days," I told him.

"I will see you both in the morning," he said and walked out. Damn, he is still so damn angry with me. Tay came running in my room, she scared the shit out of me.

"Tay, what the hell is wrong with you?" I yelled holding my damn chest.

"Girl, I saw the grim reaper leave, and I wanted to make sure your ass was amongst the living! Every time you get close to this nigga my left eye start jumping. That's not good, I'm telling you, you need to keep one eye open at all times when you are around his ass. But noooooo, yo' ass want to be up in this bitch like you sleeping fucking beauty. Keep on and you gone be a dead fucking beauty!" Taymar fussed, and I fell out laughing.

"Tay how did you know I was sleep?" I asked her.

"You forgot about that hole in the wall near the door that Grammy never got fixed. Well, you can call me peep a Tay round this bitch! I went from peeping in the hole to sticking the barrel of grandma shotgun in the hole. I wanted to make sure that shit fit! Girl, when he was standing over you, I thought that fine nigga was gone choke the spit out yo' ass! I'm tired sus, watching yo' damn back done made my ass crazy!" she laughed.

"Tay, you been crazy you don't need no help in that department. What time are you going out?" I asked her still laughing at her crazy self.

"He said he will be here at seven, so I need to go get dressed," she responded and left the room. I decided to take a shower and pack our things for our flight in the morning.

Chapter Seventeen

LAW

$\mathcal{I}$ had just got home, and I was standing here letting Shan know that I was going to Miami. She was not taking the shit well at all.

"What the fuck do you mean, you are going to Miami?" Shantel asked.

"Shantel, she hid my son from me, I don't trust her to go and come back. I need to make sure she comes back with him. I need to know that he will be a part of my life!" I yelled.

"First of all, you don't even know if he is your son! But you just gone hop on a plane and follow them to Miami. If you are going to Miami, then so am I!" she yelled.

"No, you're not going with me. I don't want to piss her off or make this shit crazier. Did you forget the damn insults you threw at her? Trust me, baby, let me handle this so that we can get back to preparing for our beautiful day. I love you, Shantel you can trust that every move I make, you're in the forefront of that. I'm going to get him tested, but in my heart of hearts, I know that he is my son," I pulled her in for a kiss.

"Okay, I trust you! I just don't trust her lying ass," she stated.

"Shantel, I got this," I responded.

"You do know we are getting married this weekend coming up! My family is coming in, are we still putting some of them in the penthouse?" she asked.

"Yeah, that's fine. I'm going to my shop, I will be back in a couple of hours," I told her.

"Okay," she walked up, and gave me a kiss and I headed out. I left my damn keys upstairs, so I turned to go get them.

"I'm on way now, I should be there in twenty minutes. Be ready for me, when I get there," she spoke on her phone.

"Who are you talking too?" I questioned, as I stood in the doorway. She jumped because I guess I scared her.

"Oh, that was Brittany, we were supposed to go out for a minute. She is supposed to put some new lashes on for me," she stated.

"Alright, I forgot my keys, I will see you later," I told her. She was acting strange, but I brushed the shit off. It was after eight and the shop was damn packed. The bar on the other side of the shop, had niggas damn near touching each other. I must say the way I had this shit set up was brilliant. I was bringing in so much money, I was thinking that I would open up another shop right across the damn street. Having my business down on South street was a money maker.

"What's good?" I spoke to my staff.

"Law, you had some girl come in and ask for you. I think she said her name was Cassy. Let me check she left her name and number for you to call her," Joe said, as he walked to get the number. The only Cassy I knew is the chick my pops was fucking with. But my mom beat her ass and she stopped fucking with Jax months ago. He gave me the number, and I pulled my cell out to call her.

"Hello," she answered on the first ring.

"Yo, this is Law, what's up?" I questioned.

"I can't really talk right now, but I really need to talk to you about Shantel, you need to watch out for her because...." Click.

"Hello," I spoke into the phone, and the call ended. I called her back, and her voicemail picked up. I tried calling her a few more times and I got the same thing. *What the fuck was she trying to tell me about my girl, they didn't even run in the same circle.* I spoke with my staff to let them know that I would be gone for a few days, and then I called to reschedule my appointments. I set my flight up and decided to have a couple of drinks. That bullshit ass call with Cassy was weighing heavy on my mind. I have to have a conversation with Shantel, I need to find out what she knew about this Cassy situation.

When I made it home it was a little after midnight. I packed a bag and decided to take a shower and take it down for the night. My alarm going off jolted me out of my sleep, I turned over and Shantel was knocked out. I hopped up and got in the shower, it was almost six. I decided to take an Uber instead of driving, which would save me some time. I kissed Shantel and told her I would call when I made it to Miami. About an hour had passed and I finally made it to the gate. I saw Love and Savion seated having a conversation, and I walked over to them.

"Is this seat taken?" I asked, and they both looked up.

"Dad!" Savion jumped up smiling.

"Law what are you doing here?" Love asked in confusion.

"I decided that I wanted to come with you," I responded, she placed headphones on Savion, and turned his iPad on.

"You don't trust me? That's the reason you wanted to come isn't it?!" she angrily spat.

"If you want an honest answer, NO," I told her and sat down.

"I didn't invite you; how do you know that I don't live with someone?" she questioned.

"To be honest, I don't care. I won't be staying with you; I just need to know where you are and make sure my son comes back to Philly. That's my only concern when it comes to you," I said to her. Love could be mad all she wanted but every step my son takes from this point on, I will be taking them damn steps with him.

*I*t has only been two damn days, but I was really feeling Taymar. She is funny, down to earth, fine, and had the best pussy in the fucking world. I tried to shake her off all day, it was just something about her that had a hold on my ass. I took her to dinner, and my ass had to sit right next to her instead of sitting across from her.

I knew then, she had my ass over the top gone. I had one problem and it could potentially be a big problem for me, and that was Teana. She and I fucked a few times and she said she didn't want a relationship with me. In my mind, I hadn't done anything wrong, but I felt I needed to be straight up with her. Because Tay really had me in my feelings about her ass. Our vibe was off the charts, and we just connected with each other.

I would have never thought I would be attracted to Tay.

We damn sure knew each other but It never once crossed my mind of fucking with her. When Love left, it was like we never saw any of them again. I found out that Tay was away in college, she decided that she wanted to stay in New York. I was sitting in front of Jax's house because I needed to put this nigga in his place. His housekeeper let me in and told me he was in his office.

"What's up?" he asked as he looked up.

"Why the fuck are you still pushing weight? I thought it was weed. But I found out that its more than just weed, nigga! We had a deal, but I should have known that you were full of shit. Your money is cut off, you can't be trusted," I gritted.

"You thought that I was going to let you, and my pussy ass son, stop me from getting my money! Fuck that, I met with that fine ass connect you got, and she gave me all the dope I needed. It looks like I got my territory and you have yours, don't make this shit a war. This will only hurt your mother in the end," this bitch nigga spoke, and I wanted to blow his fucking brains all over this office. I knew if I did that my mom and brother would be hurt over this.

"My mother is the only reason your bitch ass is still breathing, but don't fucking push me!" I gritted and walked out. What the fuck was Tee doing? She knew what it was with me and Jax. I hopped in my car and jumped on I476 and headed out to King of Prussia to pay her ass a visit.

She let me through the gates and was waiting at the door when I pulled up to the house.

"Why the fuck would you supply Jax?" I questioned pissed the fuck off.

"Why the fuck you coming to my house with all of that aggression? You need to bring that shit all the way down. It's none of your concern who I go in business with. If you feel threatened by Jax being back on the streets, that sounds like a personal problem to me!" This bitch stated. I was not for her bullshit tonight, she wanted to be a big dog in this street shit. She better get ready for the shit coming her way fucking with me.

"What the fuck is wrong with you, I thought we were cool?" I said to her, and she acted as if she could give two fucks.

"Us being cool doesn't have shit to do with my business," she stated.

"Say word, I got you lil' mama. Since you said that, I think we need to keep it strictly business then. I think I found someone that I would like to be exclusive with," I told her, and she adjusted that smile on her face to a frown.

"You mean that lil' bitch, Taymar. You would miss out on someone like me, fucking with a bitch like her. She has nothing, and I have everything you would ever need. I think you should rethink your decision; things could get really ugly for you and her," she threatened.

"Bitch let me tell you something, I don't give a fuck what you have! But if you ever threaten me again, I will show you who I really am. Oh yeah, if you fuck with Taymar, you will regret the day you ever met my ass!" I told her.

"You might as well go find you another supplier, our business is over!" she yelled.

"I thought business was business but fuck you and your fucking dope! Bitch!" I yelled and walked away. I was fucking pissed that she would even let this nigga Jax in. She knew what we were dealing with when it came to his ass. How the fuck did she even know about Tay? I guess I needed to beef up my security and make sure Tay was going to be alright. I dialed up Zeno because we needed to regroup and quick. I had just gotten my shipment from her a few days ago, so we were cool for a couple of months. I'm glad that I got double the amount that we normally get.

"What's up, bruh?" Zeno greeted.

"Yo, I just had a fall out with Tee. Get everybody together and meet me at the spot," I spoke.

"I'm on it," he responded, and ended the call. By the time I made it back to Philly, everyone had made it to the warehouse.

"Listen up, Tee is in business with Jax and she is pissed that I'm fucking with Taymar. She threatened me, and stopped our supply," I told them.

"Damn, that's fucked up! She letting dick cloud her judgment. I thought Tee was a hard body, why the fuck she lay down with Jax bitch ass!" Cam fussed.

"It is what the fuck it is, we need to make sure we straight. Cam beef up security and move my drugs to our safe house. I don't trust her ass, Zeno, I need you to put big Rob, Cash, and Black in the safe house with my money and dope." I hate that Tee and I were not seeing eye to eye because we really made a lot of money together.

"Yo boss, I think I may know of another connect. But we will have to make sure we dead this bullshit with Tee first," Rich stated.

"We will talk about it," I told him. If a war is what Tee wants, a war is what she will get. Fucking with me, and anyone associated with me is going to be a problem she doesn't want.

Chapter Nineteen

LOVE

e were back in Miami, and I had my car parked in the parking garage here at the airport. The funny thing is the car that Law gave me, I had a black one just like it. I had just purchased it a few days before my grandmother called me about my mom. When we made it to the car, he looked at the car and then at me and laughed.

"I see you don't really need me to upgrade your car when you upgraded already," he stated, and I popped the trunk.

"No, I'm fine over here," I said and hopped in the car. I was still pissed, and a little hurt that he didn't believe I would come back to Philly. About thirty minutes later, we arrived at my home.

"Damn, I see you living good down here. I know this neighborhood, I think we did a tour here a few years ago," he stated.

"Yes, they give tours on the boats, this is called Millionaire row, I told him as we got out of the car.

"Yeah, that's it," he replied. We made it inside the house, and Celeste was walking down the steps.

"Les! I missed you," Savi stated as he took off running over to his nanny.

"I missed you too, how was your trip?" she asked Savi with a smile.

"It was fun, look, Les," Savi stated, pointing at his father.

"Oh my god, is it...Is it really him?" she looked at me, holding her chest.

"Yeah, it's him," I told her, and Law smiled at her and introduced himself.

"Sir, it's nice to meet you, finally. Come on Papi let's go get you settled," Celeste stated, and she took Savi upstairs.

"Would you like something to drink?" I asked Law as we walked into the kitchen.

"I'm good, I don't get any of this. You talked to our son about me and made sure that he knew who I was. But why didn't you allow me to know who he was?" he asked.

"You know why, I was afraid, and I didn't want my son hurt or raised in that environment," I responded.

"You didn't even give me a chance, Love. How do you know what decisions I would have made? Especially if I had a child. All of my decisions would have been based on the well-being of my son," I told her.

"Law, I'm truly sorry. If I could change any of it. I would, but I can't change it. We will have to figure out how to make this all work. His birthday is this weekend coming up and I want him to enjoy it with both of his parents. Can we at least do that for him?" I questioned.

"What day?" he asked as he stood.

"Saturday, is everything alright?" I asked in confusion because he seemed as if something was bothering him.

"My wedding is this Saturday," he spoke.

"Oh, well I'm sure Savi will understand that. You can always spend time with him before your wedding, and when you come back from your honeymoon," I stated, feeling uneasy talking about the fact that he was getting married.

"Maybe," he replied.

"How long have you two been together?" I asked as I placed a bottled water in front of him.

"A little over three years. Shantel is a very special woman and I love her," he stated.

"That's good, I'm happy for you," I told him.

"Why did you just up and leave? What made you decide to marry Zion?" He asked.

"I wasn't thinking, I was angry with you about being in the streets. The drugs you were pushing, were the drugs that my mother was hooked on. All of that played a part in why I made the decision to leave. That night I called Zion and told him that I wanted to be with him, but I needed to know that he was serious. He flew me out to LA and we just made the decision to get married. We didn't tell anyone, we went and got married the day before the draft. I made a lot of bad decisions that I regret," I told him, just as my doorbell sounded off. I walked off to answer the door, and I knew this shit was going to go bad.

"What are you doing here?" I asked, Zion.

"Where the fuck have you been? I called your phone and you ignored my calls!" he yelled.

"Where I go is no concern of yours!" I said to him.

"I know you took your hoe ass to Philly. I bet you went looking for him, didn't you? You couldn't even love me, because you were too busy loving that nigga all these years! I asked you to give me a child, but you came up with an excuse every time I suggested it. I knew you only wanted your children by that pussy ass nigga!" he roared, and I was pulled out of the way and Law's hands were wrapped around Zion's neck.

"Say that shit to me, nigga! Get in my muthafuckin face and say what you need to say. But if you ever disrespect her again, I'm going to break your jaw!" Law roared and threw Zion to the floor.

"This is my shit nigga, my shit and all you muthafuckers can get the fuck out! I pay the bills here, for her and her bitch ass son!" he yelled and I slapped the shit out of him.

"Don't you ever talk about my fucking son! He is a little fucking boy, don't bring him into your fucked up—" I was cutoff because Law was beating the shit out of Zion.

"Law stop it, Savi is upstairs! Please stop," I cried, and he halted the beat down he was putting on Zion.

"Bitch, she doesn't need a damn thing from you, and my son damn sure don't need your fucking money!" Law roared.

"Law, this is my house his name is not on the deed. I

purchased this house. I won a large settlement in our divorce, and he is supposed to stay away from me and Savi. I have a protective order against him, he knows he's not supposed to be near me or Savi. Zion, if you report this to the police, I will show them that you were the aggressor. Cameras don't lie, now get the fuck out of my house!" I yelled, and he got off the floor.

"You can have the bitch!" were Zion's parting words along with another punch to the face from Law. I slammed the door and broke down in tears. I had been through so much shit with Zion, things that I never want to talk about.

"I'm sorry you had to hear all of that," I cried, and he pulled me into him.

"It's all good. Are you alright?" he asked me, and I pulled away from him.

"Yes, I will be fine. Zion has a bad temper and he's been that way for a long time," I sighed.

"Has he ever put his hands on you before?" he asked me, I didn't want to answer that question. But I also didn't want to lie to him.

"Yes," I responded.

"Has he ever put his hands on Savion?" he stood.

"No, he's never touched Savi. I have always protected him from the bullshit that Zion and I went through. Zion was cheating, I really didn't care what he did. Our marriage was over before it started, and I was fine with that," I smiled.

"I think I need to get to my hotel; I will call an Uber.

Would you two like to meet me for dinner tonight?" he asked pulling out his phone.

"You are more than welcome to stay here with us. We have plenty of room, and we won't disturb you," I told him.

"I don't think that would be a good idea. But I would love for Savi, to spend some time with me while we are here," he stated.

"Okay, we will meet you for dinner and I will ask Savi if he wants to stay the night with you," I responded.

"I would like that; my Uber will be here in about fifteen minutes. Is it okay if I go up and say goodbye?" he questioned.

"Yes, when you get upstairs, he is the first door on the right," I told him. Damn, we haven't been here but a couple of hours and he has gotten into some shit with Zion. But if Zion knows like I do, he won't mess with Law by going to the cops. The way Law beat his ass, I don't think he wants to mess with him at all. I feel such a relief knowing that I don't have to hold this secret in any longer. I knew that I was going to have to tell Law, to be honest. Savi was asking more and more questions about his dad. So, the time would have come, it just came sooner than I anticipated it.

Chapter Twenty

LAW

I finally made it to my hotel, and I needed to relax for a while. That shit back at Love's house really had my ass boiling over. I can't believe she was letting that nigga put his hands on her. I felt good about beating his punk ass the fuck up. I made a few calls to Shantel, but she didn't answer. A few minutes later she was calling back.

"Why didn't you answer my calls?" I asked her.

"Sorry babe, I was in the hair salon. How is everything going?" she questioned.

"Good, I'm staying at the Marriott on Biscayne Blvd," I told her.

"Okay, I have to go into the mall before I go home. Call me later tonight," she stated, I could only look at my phone and ended the call. Lately, every time I called her ass, she was rushing me off the phone. I forgot to ask her about Cassy. My phone was vibrating, and I saw that it was my brother calling.

"What up, bruh," I greeted.

"Yo, shit is all bad. I found out that Tee was serving Jax, we fell out over that shit and we fell out about Tay. But that is not all, they just found Cassy ass dead in Fairmont Park," Sin spoke.

"What?! Damn, she tried to reach me the other day. When I called her back, she said that I needed to watch out for Shantel. In the middle of our conversation, the call ended," I told him.

"Did you ask Shantel, what she had going on with Cassy?" he asked me.

"Nah, I forgot to ask her. I'm down in Miami, Love had to come take care of some shit and I was not trusting the fact that she would come back. But I'm calling Shantel and getting to the bottom of this Cassy shit," I replied.

"Yeah you do that, I'm about to pull up and see what the deal is with Tay," Sin stated.

"Nigga, how the hell you get wrapped up in Tay ass so damn quick?" I asked him.

"Bro, I thought I would never say this. My ass is so far gone over this girl, the shit was so damn good I went and talked to Ma. Bruh, I don't know what the fuck that girl got between her legs, but a nigga can't get enough of that shit! I let that fucking pussy infiltrate the empire, that shit done fucked up my dope supply. It was all worth it, though!" this nigga stated, and I burst into laughter.

"Boy, your ass is crazy!" I laughed.

"Nigga, I see why yo' ass was flipping over Love, all these years. Because if it's anything like her cousin's, that shit would've had me crazy too. You down there in Miami with her ass now, don't let that shit suck you back in!" Sin stated, and we ended the call. His statement must be true because Love's ass had a hold on me for years. Ever since she came back that shit has been trying to resurface back to the top. I'm loyal to my girl, and I guess that's all that matters. I grabbed my phone to call Shantel back.

"Hello," she answered.

"Shantel, do you know someone by the name of Cassy?" I asked her.

"No, I never heard that name before. Why?" she questioned.

"She came into the shop looking for me and left a number. I called her back, she was trying to warn me about you," I told her, and the phone got quiet.

"About me, for what? Babe, I don't know who this person is," Shantel stated.

"Alright, if you say you don't know her, then I guess you don't. I wanted to ask you about her. We good, I will call you later," I said to her and hung up. A few hours later, I was having dinner with Love and Savion. The more time I spend with this little boy, the more I learn about his smart self. When his mom said he was intelligent for his age she wasn't lying. He knew how to count in large numbers, he knew multiplication, and he could name all of the damn presidents.

"Mom, I'm sleepy," Savion spoke.

"Okay, baby, you need to eat just a little more and we can leave," Love told him.

"I think we should get the check and take him upstairs," I stated.

"Yeah, he has had a long day," Love replied. The waitress came, and I paid the bill so we could get him to bed. I picked Savion up, by the time we made it upstairs he was already asleep. I went to lay him down, and his mother changed him into his pajamas. When we agreed that he would stay the night with me, I changed my room so that we could have two bedrooms. I walked back out into the living room area and poured me a drink. A few minutes later Love walked out.

"He should be sleeping for the rest of the night," she spoke, and I could only stare at her. Damn this girl was absolutely beautiful, everything about her fine ass was perfect.

"Law," she called out.

"Yeah, I'm sorry, what were you saying?" I asked.

"I was just letting you know that Savi should be sleeping for the rest of the night," she smiled.

"Okay, great, I have a question for you. How did he get my last name? I thought I needed to sign the birth certificate in order for that to happen?" I questioned, I have a friend and he was so pissed that his kid didn't have his last name. He said he was told that he needed to be there and sign the paperwork, and he wasn't there.

"I knew the nurse, and she allowed me to sign it. There

was no way that I was going to give your son Zion's last name," she responded.

"Good! I would have been extremely pissed if that had happened," I replied.

"I think I better get home; I will check on you two in the morning." She walked to the door. But it was something that was eating at me, and I just had to know the answer.

"Is it true?" I blurted out.

"Excuse me, is what true?" she asked in confusion.

"Is what Zion said earlier true, you only wanted to have kids by me?" I stood and walked over to where she was standing. She seemed nervous all of a sudden, dropping her head looking at the floor. I took my finger and placed it on her chin lifting it so that she could look at me.

"I guess it really doesn't matter anymore, you are going to be a married man soon," she shrugged.

"I guess you're right, have a good night, Love," I smiled, and went to take my seat at the bar. If she didn't want to answer my question, I couldn't make her do it. I sipped on my drink, and she just stood there facing the door. She eventually turned to face me; I knew she was battling with herself internally.

"Yes, everything he said is true, I was in love with you. Hell, I'm still in love with you. I only wanted to have my babies by you, that's the reason I would never give him any children. I dreamed about you; I've been dreaming about you for over five fucking years. I haven't been with a man in years, because I only want to feel you inside of me. I can't put all the blame on Zion in our marriage. I guess if I was more focused on him, as my husband, he might have turned out to be a good husband to me. He would get angry and violent with me because I made sure that Savi knew his real father. I wouldn't allow our son to call him daddy. My love for you runs deep. I have never in my life loved another man like I love you. Is that being honest enough for you?" she asked, as she walked and stood in front of me.

"Damn!" was all I could say.

"I love you, Savion, I have been waiting for years to tell you that. I've missed you so much, I know I shouldn't be saying this to another woman's soon-to-be husband. I just needed to get this off my chest. Now that you're getting married, I have to find a way to get rid of these feelings I have for you. It's going to be so hard to do because all I ever wanted was you. To feel you inside of me again, to touch you," she stated, as she rubbed her finger on my lips.

I opened my mouth and she slid her finger in, as I sucked on it. Picking her ass up and quickly pinning her against the bar. We began attacking each other's lips, trying to damn near choke the life out of each other. I aggressively sucked and bit her neck, the need for her was so fucking bad. I could barely breathe; I damn near tore her shirt off trying to get her breast out as I sucked and nibbled on her nipple. My dick felt as if it was going to burst through my jeans it was so damn hard. Then it hit me like a ton of bricks! What the fuck was I doing!

"I'm sorry, I can't do this. I need you to leave. I have a

fucking fiancé that I love, and this shit isn't right. I'm so sorry, if I mislead you," I whispered, and let her down. She fixed her clothes and walked out of the room without saying a word. This shit was fucked up. How could I allow this to happen? I had a weak moment, and I could never let this happen again. I had to call my mom because this shit was getting out of hand.

"Hello," she groggily spoke.

"Ma, I almost fucked up and slept with Love," I told her.

"What! What the fuck is wrong with you and your brother! Stay away from the good pussy heifers and go the fuck to bed! Damn, you two niggas gone drive my ass insane. Listen, Shantel is going to be your wife soon. You need to figure this shit out. If you are having second thoughts, don't get married. I won't be mad at you, but son, you have to know deep down in your heart if you are making the right decision. Now with that being said, good fucking night!" she stated and hung up on my ass. I decided to have a couple more drinks and chill out for the night.

Chapter Twenty-One
SIN

A couple of days had passed since the blow-up with Tee. Things have been quiet, but that only means that some shit was about to pop off. I have a meeting in a couple of weeks with a new connect and I'm happy about that shit. Law and Love made it back to Philly a few hours ago, and the wedding was a few days away. We had the rehearsal dinner Friday night, and bachelor party I was throwing for Law. Tay and I were out having dinner.

"So, my brother is getting married on Saturday. I'm hoping you will come with me and be my date," I said to her.

"Nah, I don't like that hoe! I'm team Love, and that bitch tried my cousin. I had to put my fist all on her fucking jaw. I will meet you after the wedding is over," she replied.

"When this shit happen?" I asked her.

"The day before we hooked up at the club, Love and I was

down South street and we saw the tattoo shop. I wanted a tattoo, so we went in and found out that Law owned the place. The hoe came in and was being a bitch! So, I gave her ass something to bitch about," she shrugged as she popped a fry in her mouth.

"Damn, that shit is crazy. Are you going home tonight or are you staying with me?" I asked her.

"It doesn't matter, you ain't getting no pussy anyway, my period is on and the shop is closed until further notice," she smiled.

"I guess you better get them jaws cracking then," I laughed, and she hit me on the shoulder.

"I'm just fucking with you, my shit ain't on yet you got another week so you better do all you can. Because lil' baby coming and she doesn't play," we both burst out laughing.

"Well isn't this shit picture-perfect," Tee stated, as she walked up to our table and took a seat. Taking a fry off of my plate and eating it, I looked over at Taymar and she looked at me.

"What the fuck are you doing?" I gritted at Tee.

"Bitch, who the fuck are you?!" Taymar yelled out.

"You lucky I'm in a good mood today but make that the last bitch you call me lil' girl!" Tee told her.

"Bitch! Like the fuck I said! Why you at our table eating off my damn man plate?" Tay yelled.

"Your man? Nah, this is my man!" Tee stated, and I was fucking steaming.

"Tee get the fuck away from my table. I fucked you, I was never your fucking man," I told her.

"Oh, you one of them funky bitches, that can't keep they feelings in check. When a nigga tells you he just fucking you, believe him hoe!" Taymar stated.

"What was that?" Tee questioned, as she pulled her gun out and pointed it at Tay.

"Oh lawwwwed, this bitch got a gun, you can have him boo. The dick wasn't even that good, I don't fight over no damn man. But you pulling that damn gun on me, is another damn story. We can get this gunplay poppin' in this bitch, BITCH!" Taymar spoke, as she lifted her gun from under the table and pointed it at Tee. I was wondering why she was digging in her purse.

"Tee, if you don't get that gun out of my woman's face, I promise you, your night won't end well," I roared, and she stood.

"I see you got a spunky lil' bitch, see you around, baby," she smiled, and walked away.

"You alright, baby?" I questioned Tay.

"Get me the fuck out of here and take me home!" she screamed. I threw some money on the table and we left the restaurant. This shit with Tee was going to be a problem. I can't believe she walked up on us like that and pulled a gun out on Tay. That was going to be the last time that hoe pulled a gun on anybody. I don't fucking hit women, but this bitch was going to make me beat her ass.

"I think you should stay at my house, for a little while. I

need to make sure you will be safe," I said to Tay, as I pulled up to her house.

"You staying the fuck away from me, will also make me safe!" she yelled and jumped out of the car.

"Taymar! Come back here and talk to me!" I roared, but she kept moving until she made it inside the house. If Tee thinks for one second that she is going to fuck with me or Tay, she got another thing coming. I'm going to kill this bitch!

Chapter Twenty-Two

LOVE

I was so fucking embarrassed and hurt about what happened at Law's hotel room. The next day I dropped more clothes off for Savi and didn't say much to Law. I went and handled all of the business concerning my job and other things that I needed to take care of. We got back to Philly yesterday and today I have to meet Law at the DNA testing center. I didn't put up a fight with him, because I understood why he needed to be sure. I went to check on Tay, I heard her come in last night. But she didn't come and tell me how her date went. I knocked on the door and waited but I didn't get a response.

"She is in the kitchen, baby," Grammy said, as she came down the hall.

"Morning, Grammy, how are you feeling?" I asked her.

"I'm good, just a little tired from all of the visitors we have had. I'm glad that you and Tay are here to keep me company. That child in there talking about she's going back to New York soon," Grammy responded.

"I'm going to talk to her and see what is going on," I told her and kissed her on the cheek. I walked in the kitchen and Tay was in there bouncing her leg up and down, and texting on her phone all fast. I thought she was going to break her damn fingers.

"Tay, how was your date, boo?" I asked.

"Sus, fuck that good dick nigga! From this day on, I'm fucking ugly niggas with lil' dicks. That nigga gone have missing teeth in the front so it will be easy enough to suck on my clit! Fuck that, I'm too young to die over a nigga and his dick. Tay trying to keep it cute and stay the fuck alive! What's that shit they put on the stones when people die 'Gone but not forgotten'. My shit gone read 'Gone off the dick for no damn reason' Fuck that!" She went on and on, and I was bent over in laughter.

"Tay, what the hell happened?" I questioned because my cousin was serious about this shit.

"So, Sin and I were at dinner and the pretty bitch came walking up to the table and sat the fuck down! She was talking about how Sin her man and blah blah blah! I was getting with the bitch until she pulled out a gun on my ass! Bitch, I told that hoe to get her man, because the dick wasn't even good! If that nigga was looking for a ride or die bitch, Tay ain't it! I'm gone ride my ass back to New York and find my ugly spooky ass nigga. Ion even want to look at a fine nigga no muthafuckin' mo!" she fussed, and I swear it wasn't funny, but this girl was crazy.

"Oh my God, she pulled a whole gun on you? Yeah, I don't blame you! That shit is crazy," I told her.

"How was Miami? I heard you had a surprise with you," she smiled.

"I was pissed at first, but eventually I was fine with it. Savi enjoyed having his dad there with him. Girl why did Zion show up at the house?" I said to her.

"Law was there?" she asked me.

"Yep, and he beat his ass! Zion was talking a lot of shit about me and Savi. I slapped his ass a few times, but Law beat the shit out of that nigga," I shook my head.

"I would have given anything to see that shit. I'm glad you are alright though," she replied, just as her phone went off again.

"This nigga keeps calling me. On a serious note though, it's fucked up because I really liked him," Tay spoke, and she seemed sad about it.

"Tay, everything is going to work out. Let me go get Savi ready, we are doing the DNA testing today," I stood.

"I'm staying here until Sunday, and then I'm heading back to New York. I was hoping to see my mother, but Grammy said she left while I was out last night," Tay stated.

"Okay, maybe you can go with me on Saturday to take Savi out for his birthday. His dad will be busy getting married," I responded.

"Count me in," she replied. I smiled at her and left her

with her thoughts. I could tell that this shit with Sin was really bothering her. She was so damn excited that they had gotten together. I think I will call him and see what the problem is and what he plans to do about it. A couple of hours later, Savi and I were walking in the testing center and Law was already there waiting.

"Hey, have you been here long?" I asked him, as we took our seat.

"Nah, I just got here. Hey, lil' man, how was your night?" Law asked Savi.

"It was good dad," Savi replied with a big smile. He told his dad that it was alright to call him what he wanted to call him. Law was so surprised at how smart Savi was. I told him they wanted to boost him to the first grade, but I wouldn't let them do that. Maybe when he gets to middle school or high school. But I want him to stay in the grade that he is supposed to be in while in elementary.

"Savion Williams," the nurse called out, and Law stood and grabbed Savi's hand. I followed behind them, and she led us into this room. She swabbed both of their mouths and drew some blood.

"Savi, you are being a big boy today," I told him.

"I'm strong like my daddy, mom," he laughed.

"That's right, I need you to always be strong," Law told him and smiled. My heart was happy for both of them. About twenty minutes later we were finished and walking out of the building.

"I will be by later to pick him up, I would like to take him out for his birthday. If that's alright with you?" he asked, and I was fine with whatever he wanted to do with his son.

"Yes, it's fine," I spoke, and turned to walk away but he grabbed my hand.

"Listen, I'm really sorry about what happened in Miami. Even though I'm getting married, I would like to try and build some type of friendship with you again. I hope we can do that for the sake of our son. I don't think we should feel like we're walking on eggshells when we are around each other. Can we at least try for him?" he pointed at Savi, and I looked up at him.

"Yeah, we can," I whispered. It was killing me inside to know that in two days he was going to be married, and off-limits. For so many years I prayed for this man and loved him so deep. I don't think I would ever be the same again, now I could only pray that my heart would heal and let him go.

Chapter Twenty-Three

LAW

I stopped by my mom's house because she said she had some stuff she needed me to pick up for Shantel. I was very surprised that my mom really liked Shantel, and they got along so well. It has always been a challenge to get our mom on the same page when it came to women we dated.

"Oh, hell nawl! Let me go get my muthafuckin gun!" I heard my mom yell and walked in the kitchen.

"What's going on? Ma, why do you need your gun?" I looked from my mom to Sin waiting on one of them to answer my question.

"It's Tee, she pulled up on me and Taymar last night while we were having dinner. She threatened me and pulled a gun on Tay. Tay is not fucking with me no more, I need to get Tee ass in order, or it's going to be some shit," Sin stated.

"Fuck! Ma, you don't need to involve yourself in this shit. Tee is on another level of crazy, and she is the fucking connect. Pop has his hand in this shit, that's the reason he went to her in the first place," I told Sin.

"Now wait a minute, why do you boys always think that Jax is behind some shit?" she questioned, getting all in her damn feelings.

"Ma, Pops ain't shit and you need to stop fucking with him. That nigga is really going to fucking hurt you, and I'm going to put his ass in the dirt over you! What the hell is up with this Cassy shit? They said that girl was murdered and dumped in the park. Ma, she tried to reach out to me a couple of days before she got clipped!" I yelled.

"I don't know what happened to her, but I know your father doesn't have anything to do with it. Listen, I didn't like the hoe, but I damn sure didn't want to see her dead. Boys, I got this shit with me and Jax, I need for you to get this girl in order, Sincere. Taymar is a good girl, and she doesn't need to be mixed up in this bullshit. If you don't, I promise you, I'm going to have a talk with this girl myself! Law the bag is in the family room, tell Shantel I will call her later," she said and walked off.

"Sin you need to talk to this girl, I need your head clear by tomorrow," I told him. I left my mom's and went to pay my pops a visit.

"I knew you would be coming soon," he stated.

"Pop why are you fucking with Sin? You made a deal, and now you trying to fuck up his money! You are fucking up my damn money too, this is why I told him not to bring you in on this shit! You can't be trusted, and I'm your fucking son! Why would you want to fuck up what I have going on?!" I yelled.

"Do you think I give a damn that you are my son! Business is business, and I have to teach you young niggas that you can't fuck with me and think you're going to push me out the way. I invented this drug shit!" he roared.

"Nigga, please! You didn't invent shit, but a fucked-up group of niggas that couldn't sell a fucking dime bag of washing powder. You and those old ass niggas are played the fuck out! Find something safe to do pops! Another thing, I don't know what Cassy got into, but I can almost bet all of my fucking money I have, you are involved in that shit. If you get my mom caught up in some bullshit! I promise you this, I'm going to kill you," I told him and walked out of his office.

Something caught my eye, as I passed by his living room. It was a pair of shoes that looked just like the pair I got for Shantel when we were in Paris last year. I shrugged it off because my pops has traveled all over the world with his women. I'm sure when they made one pair, they made thousands of them. I brushed it off and walked out and headed down to my shop; I had a few appointments today. I couldn't wait to spend some time with Savion later. I knew I would have to introduce Shantel to Savion. But I've decided that I would do it when we came back from our honeymoon. It was damn near six and I needed to leave and go pick up Savion.

"I will see you tomorrow," I said to my best friend, Dax.

"Yes sir, can't wait! This is going to be the wedding of the century!" He laughed, and we dapped it up. By the time I made it to pick up Savion, it was after seven.

"Hey Law, she is in the back and Savi is in the room talking to Grammy," Tay smiled.

"Everything cool with you? Sin told me what happened." I wanted to make sure she was good. I knew that her and Love were not used to all this bullshit.

"Yeah, I'm good. I just can't get caught in none of his shit. I'm actually going back to New York in a few days," she replied.

"Let me know if you need anything, I will have a talk with him. It was good to see you again; we haven't had much time to hang out. Maybe when you come back to visit," I told her.

"Yeah, that would be great," she replied. I walked to the back and knocked on the door. I didn't get a response, so I opened the door and got the shock of my fucking life! Fuck!

"I'm sorry," I stated and closed the door back.

"What's wrong?" Tay asked with a smirk on her face.

"Nothing," I replied, just as Love opened the door.

"I'm sorry about that, I knocked but I didn't hear you say anything," I said to her, as I walked in and she shut the door. I don't think I'm going to ever get that image out of my fucking head. She was fucking beautiful with clothes on, and just as beautiful in her naked glory.

"It's okay, will you be bringing him back tonight?" she questioned.

"No, we will be staying at my apartment. I will bring him back in the morning," I told her.

"Alright, here is his bag," she handed it to me and opened the door. Savion was walking out of the room.

"Are you ready, son?" I asked him.

"Yes, I'm ready. I love you mom, no crying," he said to his mother.

"Crying, are you alright?" I looked at her.

"Yes, I'm fine, I love you too, Savi. Have fun with your dad, and I will see you tomorrow," she kissed him, and we left out. I truly hoped that Love and I could build some type of friendship. She was indeed my best friend at one point, and I knew that we would never get back to that place again. But I wanted to be friends with her, I damn sure could use one.

Chapter Twenty-Four

SIN

I have been calling Tay repeatedly all damn day, she has ignored every call. I sent her texts, and the only thing she would write back was to leave her the fuck alone! I was sitting at Tee's gate waiting for her to open it the hell up. When I made it out front, she was standing at the door naked. *This bitch has completely lost her fucking mind!*

"Yoo, what the fuck is wrong with you?!" I yelled as I walked up on her.

"What the fuck is wrong with you, you fuck me and think that you can just stop. No, Sincere it doesn't work that way, you not gonna just play with me and think that shit is cool. I waited fucking five years to see what you were about, and you fuck me a few times and then go hop on the next hot pussy! Fuck you, Sin!" she screamed.

"We were just fucking, now you're following me around

and shit acting all damn crazy! Pulling a gun out on my girl, that shit is not fucking cool! I don't play games, if we are fucking that's it we just fucking! I gave you the opportunity to tell me what it was. You made your choice, that gave me options to do what the fuck I wanted to do. Now I'm going to say this and I'm not going to repeat myself: stay the fuck away from Tay and stay the fuck away from me!" I roared.

"Fuck that bitch, she lucky I didn't blow her fucking brains out at that table!" she screamed, and I pulled my gun out placing it to her head.

"Keep fucking talking, and I will blow your shit out right here in this fucking hall. Stop fucking with me and take this L! Don't get in the fire if you can't take the fucking heat!" I gritted.

"I don't take L's, now get the fuck out of my house!" she yelled.

"You heard what the fuck I said," I told her, and walked the fuck out. This shit with her was going to end badly. I could feel that shit in my spirit, I should have just killed the bitch and be ready for whatever comes my way. My phone was going off, and Law's name popped up.

"What's up bro?" I greeted.

"Yooo, did you know that Tay was leaving?" he asked.

"Leaving, what the fuck you mean she is leaving?" I questioned.

"I was over there a couple of hours ago, and she answered the door. We talked for a minute, and she told me she was going back to New York," he said, and I told him I would call him back. I pulled up in front of Ms. Josephine's house and walked up to ring the bell. It took a few minutes for someone to answer the door.

"How are you, Ms. Josephine, is Tay home?" I asked her.

"Yeah, she is in her room, give me one second," she replied. A few minutes later, Tay came walking out with a frown on her face.

"Why are you here?" she was pissed, and I couldn't blame her. With all that has happened, I would be pissed as well. But she needed to know that I would protect her with my life. I have only been fucking with her for a little while, and I have this connection with Tay. I want this girl in my life, so her leaving is not going to happen.

"Tay, I'm sorry, baby. I was never in a relationship with her. The girl has lost her fucking mind, but I will never let anything happen to you," I told her, as I pulled her into me trying to kiss her. She turned her face and I kissed her cheek.

"Sin, I don't do drama and I damn sure don't argue over dick. Obviously, the girl can't take rejection, which means she's unstable. I don't have time for that shit, I think it's just best that we don't fuck with each other," Tay stated.

"Nah, that's not gonna work for me," I whispered, as I began sucking and licking on her neck.

"Mmmmmm, shit! Mmmmm mmmmm, get your tongue off of me. You trying to get me caught up, and—" her words were cut off, as I slipped my hand down her shorts and began massaging her pussy.

"Damn, this pussy is wet," I gritted, and that shit gripped my fingers.

"Oh shit, mmmmmm," she moaned, and I pulled my hand out of her shorts, lifting her up in my arms carrying her ass out the door. I didn't give a damn what she was talking about she was going home with me tonight.

"What are you doing?" she laughed.

"Fuck that, I need to be inside of you and I was ready to bend your ass over Ms. Josephine's couch and fuck the shit out of you," I said, as I put her in the car and then hopped in and sped off. We made it to my crib in fifteen minutes flat, we couldn't even get in the house good. I was ripping that lil' shit she had on off of her ass. I crashed my lips onto hers, as I sucked and pulled on her tongue. I trailed kisses down her body to her thighs, spreading her legs apart. I dived in sucking and licking on her clit.

"Ohhhhh fuck, suck that shit!" Tay moaned out, as she grind her pussy into my mouth. Damn, her moaning and the way she moved under me had me ready to burst. I slid my tongue in and out of her, and then applied pressure as I sucked on her clit.

"Fuckkkkkkkk! I'm about to cum," she screamed. I immediately lifted and slid inside of her. Her pussy just gripped my shit, and I lost all control. I went crazy inside her pussy. I pulled out of her and began slapping my dick across her clit.

"Ohhhh shit, stop playing with me and fuck me!" she screamed.

"Tell me you gonna stay with me, and let daddy handle this bitch!" I told her as I rubbed my dick on her pearl.

"Shit, I'm going to stay ahhhhhhh! Fuck me, baby," she moaned out, and I rammed my dick in her giving her long deep strokes. I was fucking this girl so damn good and hard It felt like I was going to split her ass in two.

"Come ride this dick!" I gritted, as I pulled out of her and she mounted me. Tay was a pro when it came to fucking. I swear I wanted to choke the shit out of her for fucking other niggas before me! She had to learn this shit from somewhere.

"Shit, ride this dick, baby!" I gritted; this girl was fucking the hell out of me.

"Mmmmmm I'm about to pull that cum right up outta yo' ass, shit!" she screamed as she applied pressure grinding up and down my damn dick. When she started screaming and cummimg on my dick, I completely lost it, releasing all in her shit. I pulled her up from the couch and carried her into the bedroom. All night, I put my stamp all over Taymar. She belonged to me and that shit was never going to change. If she had any thoughts on leaving me, I think I just fucked those thoughts right out of her fucking memory bank.

Chapter Twenty-Five

LOVE

ay and I decided to hang out at club Lux and have a few drinks. I'm so glad that my Grammy said she would watch Savi for me. I needed this outing; I have been stressed the fuck out. Ever since we came back from Miami, Zion has been calling and texting me. One minute he is saying he still loves me, and the next minute he is threatening my life. If he keeps the shit up, I'm going to report his ass. I can't even go back down that road with his ass.

"I can't believe you and Sin have decided to be exclusive. I'm happy for you Tay, you deserve happiness," I told her.

"Yes, he said he got me and I'm trusting him on that," she stated.

"I believe he does," I smiled at her.

"So, how are you feeling, knowing that Law is getting married tomorrow?" she asked me.

"I can only accept it, I messed that up. It's time for me to move on, and open my heart up for love," I shrugged. I'm just not sure where to start, and who to start with. I guess God will send him to me because I'm damn sure not going to search for Mr. Right.

"I can't agree more cousin, you definitely deserve happiness. I can't wait to see your heart smile again. Ohhhh shit, look up in VIP," Tay said, as she nodded in the VIP section. Law and a bunch of other guys were walking into the section.

"Shit, Tay I thought Sin said they were going out for his bachelor party?" I asked her.

"He did, but he never said where they were going. I didn't know they were coming here," she stated, as she pulled her phone out and started texting. A few minutes later Sin, walked up to the bar.

"Hey ladies, y'all come up and join us," he spoke.

"I'm good, Tay you can go up if you want to go," I told her.

"Babe, we cool down here. Go celebrate with your brother," Tay said to Sin.

"Come and let me introduce you to my friends, and you can come right back," Sin told her.

"L, I will be right back," she stated and walked off with Sin. *Claim* by DSVN came blasting through the speakers. I was gyrating in the chair grooving to the music when I felt the presence of someone beside me.

"Hey beautiful, how are you tonight?" this guy asked as he sat next to me at the bar.

"Hi, I'm good," I spoke, as I turned to look at him.

"Love!" he stated, excitedly.

"Gio, Oh my God! It has been a very long time. How are you?" I asked him. Gio and I went to school together. He was drafted into the NFL and the last I heard he was playing for the Seahawks.

"I'm good, beautiful! Did you move back to Philly? I thought you married Zion's punk ass," he laughed. Gio and his crew couldn't stand Zion and his crew in school. They always got into some shit and was ready to rip each other's heads off.

"Zion and I got a divorce a few years ago, I still live in Miami. I'm just here for a few months for personal reasons."

"What are you doing here?" I asked.

"I'm here visiting the Eagles organization; they want to sign me. I'm going to be a free agent in a few weeks," he replied.

"Oh, that's great, Gio! I pray that it's a sweet deal for you," I smiled at him.

"Love, can I talk to you for a minute?" I heard Law's voice say.

"Gio, excuse me for a minute," I told him, and got up and stepped to the side to see what Law wanted with me.

"Hey what's up?" I questioned.

"Why are you down here talking to this nigga, when we are all up in VIP?" he angrily spat.

"I'm sorry, I don't think it's any of your concern. Your only concern should be Is the woman you plan to marry tomorrow," I stated and attempted to walk away but he pulled me back into him.

"Yo, my man, don't handle the lady like that," Gio said to Law, as he stood up. I knew if I didn't get a handle on this shit it was going to be a damn mess.

"Nigga, don't address me unless I decide to address your ass!" Law stepped to him.

"Gio, it's alright," I stood in between the two of them.

"Gio, come on man, let's go. We don't need the press all over this," a guy walked over trying to pull him away.

"Yeah, listen to your homie, playboy!" Law stated, and Gio charged at him. Law hit him before he could even get in his face good. That one hit sent Gio crashing to the floor and I was on my knees trying to help him up. I was snatched up and carried up the stairs and into an office.

"Put me the fuck down! What the fuck is wrong with you?" I screamed on his ass.

"What the fuck is wrong with you?! Instead of smiling in some nigga's face, shouldn't you be home with our son!" he roared, just as someone started banging on the door.

"Loveeeee, if you need help, tap your foot twice!" Tay yelled out.

"I'm fine, Tay," I told her.

"Bitch you didn't look fine, the way he was swinging yo' ass around like you was a damn ragga muffin! Law, I know who you are, and where yo' brother lives! Don't fuck with me!" she yelled.

"Our son Is fine with my grandmother! Don't fucking worry about who the fuck I talk too, touch, kiss, or fuck for that matter. I'm not your concern!" I screamed as I was being pushed into a wall.

"If you ever let another man touch you, he will be a dead muthafucka!" he gritted, as he crashed his lips into mine. Sliding my dress up and ripping my thong off, he lifted me in the air, as I wrapped my legs around his neck. He slid his tongue across my pearl latching on sucking, as he sucked life into my ass. What the fuck was really going on with us and why couldn't I fight the feeling to stay the fuck away from this man? Everything about this was wrong, and we knew it. I just couldn't stop it from happening, I wanted him just that bad.

"Ahhhhhhh," I moaned, as he applied pressure sticking his long tongue in and out of my walls. I felt like I was going crazy, I was about to lose control grinding on his tongue. All of a sudden, he stopped and held onto me for a minute. He pulled me down and placed me on the floor. I just stood there stuck not understanding what the fuck just happened. He looked at me once more and walked out of the room!

"Love, are you alright?" Tay asked as she ran inside.

"I can't believe he just did that!" I screamed out mad as hell.

"Did what?" she questioned.

"He was licking on my damn pussy, and just walked out!" I said to her.

"Oh, hell nawl! That nigga needs to get back here and finished the job! Do he know that yo' ass ain't had sex since Eve bit that damn apple? Now you need to bite on his ass, the forbidden damn tree! Fuck that! You are just gone be a home-wrecking hoe tonight! Fuck that bitch, I don't like her funky ass no damn way," Tay fussed.

"Tay, I'm good, let's get the fuck out of here," I told her. When we walked back down to the club, Law was giving me a deadly stare down. We walked outside, and I got in my car. Tay said she was going home with Sin tonight.

"Text me when you get to the house," she said, and I pulled off. I couldn't do anything but cry, I just broke down and let all of the years thinking about him and loving him out! When I made it back to Grammy's house, I just sat in the car because I needed to let it all out. I don't know if I can stay here. I think it might be best if I went back to Miami, and he can just come and see Savi. I guess that wouldn't help the situation, I placed a call and waited for her to pick up.

"Hello," Ms. Naomi answered.

"I'm sorry to bother you this time of night, but I really need to talk to you," I cried.

"Come on over baby, I will send you the address," she stated. I put my car in drive, and I drove off. When I made it to her house, I got out and rang the bell. She opened the door and grabbed my hand pulling me in the house.

"I know what loving a man like him can do to you, baby. I have been doing that shit for years. I've watched women come and go; I think for me I just got comfortable with the way things are with Jax. My boys think it's Jax that is doing me wrong, but it's the other way around. I don't want that type of relationship with Jax, I'm just there for the damn sex and money. Being in relationships, and marriage is just too damn overrated for me. He's free to do what he wants, and I'm damn sure free to do what I want to do. That's just me, and what works for me. I know you love my son, and deep down I believe he loves you too. But he's marrying Shantel, and there is nothing that you can do about it now," Ms. Naomi stated.

"I know, I'm just so hurt, I can't even express to you the amount of pain I feel. I know it's my fault, and I know I'm dead wrong for what I did to him. But how do I get past the feelings I have for him, and move on?" I asked her.

"I know it seems hard now, but you have to let go. You will find a man that is going to love you through it all! He's out there just for you, whatever God wanted you to have he will place it at your feet. All you have to do is pray on it and wait on it! I'm saying all of these encouraging words for you, and it's all true. Naomi just wasn't built like that, girl, I said fuck love a long damn time ago. But don't you give up on it," We both burst out laughing.

"Thank you, and I'm so very sorry that I kept Savi away. I will never be able to make this up to you. But I promise I won't keep him from you," I told her.

"Oh, I know you won't. Because I might have to beat that ass the next time," she laughed and reached over to hug me. We talked for a few more minutes, and then I left to go get in my bed. I was so pissed at Law but talking to his mom calmed me down.

Chapter Twenty-Six
LAW

I don't know what the fuck is wrong with me! Seeing Love talk to that nigga had my ass ready to rip his fucking head off. The way I treated her was wrong, and I know I needed to apologize to her. When she left the club, I left as soon as Tay came back in the building. I was sitting across the street from her watching her sit in the car. I saw her holding her face in her hands and wiping her eyes. I knew she was crying, and that shit tore me up inside.

Ever since Love came back into the picture my heart-strings have been pulling me into a fucking mess. I knew I still had feelings for her, but there was no way that I would ever hurt Shantel. She sat in her car for a few minutes and drove off, I decided not to follow her. Whatever she had going on was her business. I headed home, Shantel, was staying at a hotel downtown with her bridal party. I walked into our bedroom and almost tripped over something in the middle of the floor.

I turned the lights on, and it was a pair of Shantel's shoes. I walked over and picked them up, and it was the same pair of shoes that I saw at my father's house. The shit with the shoes was strange as hell. First, I see the same pair at my dad's crib, and oddly enough Shantel's pair was in the middle of the floor. *Why the fuck these shoes keep popping up!* I took them to her closet and placed them on the floor. I walked into the bathroom so that I could take a shower. Once I took care of my hygiene I crawled in bed and just laid there in the dark. I had to really think about my life and be clear that this woman is for me. *Is she the woman I want to spend the rest of my life with? If I had to give an answer tonight, I would have to say that she was.* I picked up my phone and sent a text to Love.

Me: It seems that I have been apologizing to you a lot lately. But this apology needs to happen. There is no excuse for what I did and said to you tonight. I was in my feelings, and I shouldn't have been. You were right I had no right to question you. I hope that you will forgive me, and we can move past this and raise our son.

Love: Fuck you! Now that your soul is clear, enjoy your wedding! Damn I really fucked this up, we were on our way to having some type of truce and now we've taken a few steps back. I even tried getting her to let Savion come to the wedding, but we both decided that it was his birthday and he should enjoy that. I plan on taking my baby boy his birthday gifts tomorrow morning before I head to my hotel to get ready for my big day.

The next morning, I walked downstairs to leave, and I saw the mail sitting on the counter. One of the letters was from the DNA office. I opened it up and read their findings. It stated that Savion was 99.9% my son, and I couldn't help but smile. I called my mother, and she answered after a couple of rings.

"Good morning, son," my mother greeted me.

"Mom, he's my son!" I said excitedly.

"Boy, I told you he was yours. I don't know why you went and took that damn test. Congratulations, today you have the joy of knowing that you have a son, and you are getting married. I'm proud of you Savion, you did everything the right way. You found a way to make millions and now you have your own family. I will see you at the wedding," she stated, we said our goodbyes and ended the call. I was out the door around nine and was now waiting for someone to answer the door.

"Well, if it ain't Mr. Lickums," Tay smart ass said.

"Where is Love, smart ass?" I asked her.

"They're not here. Love took him out for breakfast this morning. Law, do me a favor, give that girl a break. You have no idea what she has been through all those years loving you. I know she fucked up, but don't do her like that. I hope that I can be half the woman that she is one day. I know you loved her, and she realizes how bad she fucked up. But you can't keep fucking with her, you've moved on. Now it's time for her to do the same, I pray she finds someone to love her, and give her the life she deserves. I pray the same for you, I wish you many blessings over your marriage to hoeella," she laughed, and I had to laugh at her statement.

"Thank you, can you give these to Savion when he gets back?" I asked her.

"Yeah, I got you," Tay said, and I turned to leave. It was showtime, and I had so much shit to do before three.

Chapter Twenty-Seven

SIN

*E*verything was moving well for us in the streets, we were good on the supply and I would be meeting with my new connect next week. I had plans to still open up shop out on the West coast. My crew was setup out in LA, and just waiting for me to give the green light. Tay was my woman, and that shit felt amazing. It feels funny to be tied down to one woman, after being single for so long. I'm loving it, and I want her ass with me all the time.

I know she has a life in New York, something is going to have to change because I need her with me. I'm not sure how she is going to feel about that. I plan on talking to her tonight about it, but today it's all about my brother. Shantel is cool but to be honest, I would have preferred him being with Love. He has been loving that girl for a long ass time, and to see him settle is just wrong in my eyes. Love did some really messed up shit, but I know that he still loves her.

I watched that shit at the club go down, and I knew at that point he was still in love with L. There was no need to even talk to him about it, I knew exactly what it was hittin' for. I was on my way out the door, so I could get to the hotel. I had a miss call from Cash, and I dialed him back.

"Yo boss man, you need to get to the safe house! We got hit last night, and it's fade to Black!" he stated.

"What the fuck you mean?! Fuckkkkkk! I'm on my way," I roared, and ended the call. I rushed out to my safe house. When I made it there, the rest of my crew was already inside.

"Where is Black, and how much of my shit is gone!" I roared.

"They moved Black out already. All the dope is gone, but they didn't touch the money," Cash stated. There was no way in hell they could touch the money. I had a fireproof vault installed for my money.

"Boss, there was a note left behind," Zeno handed me the note.

Hey Baby,
Keep fucking with me and your bitch will be next!
Hugs & Kisses.

On everything I love, I'm killing this bitch!

"Clean this shit up and transport my money out of here! Zeno I will send you the address, stay with my fucking money until it's locked away," I told him and walked out. Once my brother's day is over, I'm going to take care of this crazy bitch!

When I made it back to the city I went straight to the hotel. The barber was there cutting Law's hair, my bro looked just as stressed as my ass was.

"You ready for this, bro?" I dapped him up.

"Give us a minute," he told his barber.

"What's wrong?" I questioned.

"I fucked up! I almost slept with Love," he said.

"Almost! Nigga, you didn't hit it?" I looked at him.

"No, I didn't, I took it kind of far. I definitely cross the line, but I didn't fuck her. Eventually it hit me, and I pulled away from her. It was wrong for me to lead her on, and it wasn't the first time that this shit has happened. Which lets me know that I need to stay the fuck away from her. I also need to be honest with Shantel. I love that girl too much to lie to her," this dumb ass responded.

"First of all, you can get on your knees and ask for forgiveness. Nigga, you ain't Usher, trying to give out fucking confessions and shit! This is your wedding day, maybe you should be asking yourself if you're sure you want to marry Shantel," I said to him.

"I already did that shit, and yes I do. I think it was just the fact that I had so much love in my heart for L, but that time has come and gone, and I fell in love with Shan. I apologized to Love; I just feel bad that I reacted the way I did," he stated.

"You apologized, and you say you love Shantel. Let that shit go, keep this shit between me and you! Let's go get you married, so I can go kill this bitch, Tee," I told him.

"Nigga, what the fuck happened now?" he questioned.

"She hit the safe house and got all of our bricks; the bitch had the nerve to leave me a fucking note!" I told him.

"Did she get our bread?" he stood; I knew he was pissed.

"Nah! Nobody can get in that vault, I'm having the money moved as we speak," I responded.

"Good, but I told you to handle this bitch! I would hate to step back into the game and get my hands dirty. She's getting too reckless, all over some dick she no longer has access too. What the fuck!" he spoke.

"I got this, let's just enjoy your day," I told him, and a few minutes later the barber was back in the room.

"You better have it, because this shit can get ugly real fast," he replied.

"I'm going downstairs to see what the fuck they have to eat. Why you don't have any food in this bitch anyway?" I asked him.

"Nigga, I fed y'all asses enough last night, and I'm feeding you tonight. Order some damn room service and leave me the hell alone," Law fussed.

"Why the hell y'all in this bitch looking dry? Let's get this fucking party started," Dax came in the room ready to pop some bottles. We sat around until it was time to get to the venue, where the wedding was being held.

Chapter Twenty-Eight

LOVE

I felt a pain in my heart, and I knew it was because the man that I was in love with was getting married today. Even though I had that talk with Ms. Naomi, I was still feeling some type of way about all of this. I had a feeling that he was going to try and come see Savi this morning. So, I got him up early and took him out for breakfast. I just didn't have the energy to deal with Law today. Nor did I want to see him.

When we made it back to Grammy's house, Savi had all of these gifts that his dad had left for him. I mean he had clothes, toys, sneakers, and Law got him every gaming system they damn had in the store. Law told me I had his son dressing like a square, with all these damn clothes and different designer tags. Savi's square days were over, I always thought my son dressed cute. He was so excited about what his dad had gotten for him, I was happy just seeing him smile.

"Cuz, everything is going to be alright. We can always go down there and break that shit up! You go in there and get your fucking man, and I can beat that manly looking bitch the fuck up! Never mind, I was joking, I just had a flashback of Law tossing yo' ass up like you were a two-dollar hoe," Tay said, and I fell out laughing. She was always there to lift my spirits when I felt down.

"I felt so bad for Gio, I wish I knew how to get in touch with him to check on him," I told her.

"You should feel bad, that nigga didn't even have a chance. He needs to stick to what he does best and that's run them niggas over on the football field. He charged at Law like he was about to run a play. I was sitting there like nigga nooooo, you about to run into a goon with a gun! They work differently, but when Law gave his ass that power punch! Girl, that nigga went down in 0.1 seconds. Just no if you get with him, he can't protect you!" we both fell out laughing so damn hard, it took us a few minutes to get it together. Tay's ass was crazy, but she was right. Law was a different type of dude.

"Girl, you are crazy! I really think I should check on him," I said to her.

Just think is there anybody you know from your school days that could get you his number?" she asked.

"Ummm, yeah, let me text Jason, he may be able to get it. We keep in touch and he was on the football team," I told her, as I sent Jason a text.

"Girl, I don't know how we got messed up with these good dick niggas! Good dick will fuck yo' life up, especially if the good dick bastard knows how to use it! I think we should go find us a good dick anonymous class, and if that shit doesn't exist, we can start one up and teach these bitches how to survive from having too much good dick! But first, we have to learn how to survive our damn self! Because the good dick nigga I'm fucking with still got my life fucked up, off the good dick!" She went on and on, and I was laughing so damn hard at her ass.

"Ohhhh shit, he sent it to me!" I smiled and dialed the number.

"Yeah, who is this," he spoke.

"Gio, it's me, Love, I was worried about you and wanted to check on you."

"Hey Love, I'm good baby, the nigga caught me off guard but I'm good," he stated.

"That nigga ain't catch him off guard! That nigga just got knocked the fuck—" Tay whispered but I cut her off.

"I'm glad to hear that, I'm so sorry that happened to you all because of me," I told him.

"Make it up to me, have dinner with me," he said, and Tay jumped up throwing her hands in the air. Trying to get my attention, I asked him to hold on one minute. "What?" I asked her. "If you going to accept his offer, ask him can y'all go on a date in another city. Because he won't be safe in Philly, ion even think he needs to take that deal you said he was working on. Philly not a safe place for him," she laughed.

"Girl shut yo' ass up! I laughed. I thought about it for a minute and decided why the hell not. I think is the time that I did something for me, going on a date with Gio won't hurt.

"That sounds nice, what about tomorrow night?" I asked him.

"Tomorrow night is fine, send me your address so I can pick you up," he said.

"Let's just meet somewhere, I think that would be best," I replied.

"I will text you the time and place," he responded, and we ended the call.

"Yesssssss bihhhh! Now let's hope the nigga don't have the good dick syndrome. Because we know his ass got the fine as hell Syndrome, Shit!" She shrugged.

"Girl, auntie dropped your ass on the head when she had you! Come on, and let's get dressed we have a fun day planned with my baby boy," I laughed, and we went to get ready for our day out with Savi. A couple of hours later we were walking around Old City across from the Renaissance Hotel.

"Damn, look at all the limos, and those fine ass men getting into them," Tay pointed out. When I looked up, Law was standing by a limo, smiling talking to Sin. They both got in the Limo, and eventually the cars pulled off.

"He looked happy," I whispered, as the tears filled my eyes. Tay wrapped her arms around me.

"He is marrying the wrong woman, his creation that God intended for him to have is standing right here with me," she said.

"Boo, what you know about God?" I laughed.

"Hoes know the lawwd. I pray to the good lawwd every night, asking him to remove all the good dicks from the world, so I can live a peaceful life!" She fell out laughing.

"You are going straight to hell! How are you using the lord and good dick in the same sentence?" I questioned, shaking my head. I'm glad we were talking low enough for Savi not to hear this conversation. My mind drifted back to Law, I wish him the best and hope he has many good years with his new wife. I must say Shantel is a very blessed woman to have a man like him.

Chapter Twenty-Nine

LAW

*W*e had just arrived at the venue where the wedding and reception was going to take place. When we walked in my mother was standing by the door waiting on us. I wasn't nervous earlier, but I think my nerves are working on my ass now. The crazy part is the only thing I could think about was Love, and my son.

"Awww, you all look so handsome!" She smiled, as she hugged me and Sin.

"Thanks mom, you look beautiful as well," I kissed her on the cheek.

"I'm just so full of joy, I can't believe my baby boy is getting married," she cried just as my pops walked up. I started not to invite his ass, but I knew that my mom would have a damn fit.

"Congratulations, son, I hope we can put our differences

aside and enjoy the day! For your mother's sake," my pops stated.

"I appreciate that I think we should," I told him, and gave him a hug. He was about to say something to Sin, and this fool walked away. I chuckled because my brother just didn't give a damn. Sin's dad was never in his life, and I felt bad about that. For a while, Jax stepped up to the plate and helped our mother with Sin. But I knew that was just to stay on mom's good side, he didn't give a fuck about my brother, and we both knew it. Hell, I don't think he really gives a fuck about me. That's why Sin treats him the way he does.

"He will be alright, he has a lot on his plate right now," I said to the both of them. The wedding planner walked up and pulled me away. She wanted to show me where the guys and I would be until the wedding started. I pulled out my phone and called my son, I wanted to wish him a happy Birthday. Because Love never called me when she got back home. I had a feeling that she was still pissed off and wanted to avoid me. She had to know that I was going to try and come see Savion.

"Hello," Love answered.

"Hey, I wanted to say Happy Birthday to my son," I told her.

"One second, he is playing a game with Tay. We brought him to Dave and Busters," she stated.

"That's cool, I hope he's having a good time," I heard her call out his name, and a few minutes later he got on the phone.

"Hi, daddy," he spoke.

"Happy Birthday, lil' man, are you having fun?" I asked him.

"Yeah, mommy got me lots of gifts and I got lots of gifts from you!" he responded.

"I'm glad you're having fun; I will see you in a week. I love you, son," I told him.

"I love you too." The call ended, I assumed that Love hung up.

"Bro, it's time!" Sin smiled, and I stood up to go marry this beautiful woman I had waiting for me. Shantel was so excited because her mother, father, and a few of her cousins had come in for the wedding. We walked in and took our places, and it was absolutely beautiful. The wedding had started, and my heart was beating all crazy. My father walked my mother in, and she was already in tears. After the bridesmaids and the groomsman walked in the music started playing, and everybody stood.

Shantel and her father began walking down the aisle. Damn, this was the woman I've decided to spend the rest of my life with. When they stopped and her dad gave her away, she stepped up beside me and the pastor started the ceremony. About an hour later, Shantel and I were married! She was finally my wife, and I loved her for sticking by me during the lowest time in my life. When I met her, I was still going through the motions about Love. The more time we spent together, the more the pain in my heart eased. We walked out of the ceremony as husband and wife and everyone was cheering and clapping.

"Babyyyy, we did it!" She smiled, as I bent down and kissed her lips.

"We did it, I love you, Mrs. Williams," I said to her.

"I love you too, baby," she smiled.

"Congrats, to you both," Sin stated, he gave us both a hug.

"Ohhh sweetheart you were beautiful! Congratulations, Savion, you take care of my daughter," my mother in law Krystal said.

"Always," I replied. They had us in a holding room, while they got all the guests over to the reception. Our wedding party and my mother was in the room with us.

"Shantel, are you changing now, or do you want to change after your first dance?" my mother asked her.

"I think I will wait until after the first dance and dinner," Shantel replied, as she took a glass of wine off of the table.

"Okay, everyone we are ready to go in. So, I will have them announce you as Mr. & Mrs. Savion Jaxon Williams and then you two can walk in," the planner stated.

"It's Savion Jaxon Williams Sr," I corrected her.

"Savion does it really matter? You don't know that he's your son yet," Shantel snapped.

"Actually, I do know that he's my son, and yes it does matter. The test results came in the mail, and he's my son," I said to Shantel.

"Oh, that's great, now I have to deal with the baby mama from hell," she pouted.

"Shantel we will get through this, let's just enjoy our

wedding day," I told her, we walked out of the room and I know she was in her feelings about Savion. But she would have to deal with it, my child would always come first in my life. I know they say the spouse must come first, but I'm from the new school and my kid trumps everything and everybody! We were having our first dance; once it was over, we sat down to have dinner.

"How are you feeling about being a married man?" Sin asked me.

"I'm good, glad this wedding shit is over. I can't wait until I get on this honeymoon and spend some time with my wife," I told him.

"I'm happy for you, bro, I thought yo' ass was going to pass out for a minute there. But you held that shit together," he laughed.

"I thought the same damn thing," I told him, as we sat back and enjoyed our dinner. After Sin got up and did his best man speech. It was time to party and mingle, I was ready to leave. But I knew Shan would have a damn tantrum if we didn't stay until it was over. We had a suite upstairs for the night, and we were leaving for Aruba in the morning.

"Baby, I'm going to get out of this heavy ass dress and change into my reception gown. I will be back soon, I'm ready to get my drink on and party," she giggled.

"You need my help?" I winked at her.

"No, I'm good. We are saving all that for tonight. I will be right back," she stated and left to go change.

"Bro, I'm going to pick up Tay and come right back. I

talked her into coming down to the reception I should only be about thirty minutes," Sin stated.

"Alright, but hurry back, I'm sure we have more pictures to take and it should take about that time for Shantel to get dressed and get back into the ballroom," I replied, and he took off out the door. I went to the bar to get me a drink and talked with some of my guests. I looked at my watch and it was taking Shantel a long time to get changed.

"Savion, where is Shantel? I think we should cut the cake soon," my mother said, as she walked up to me.

"She went to get dressed; I will go get her. She should have been back by now," I responded.

"Come on, I will go with you," she said, and we walked off back to the holding room they had set up for me and Shantel. When I opened the door, all I saw was red!

"Oh, my fucking god! Nooooo, I know this dirty bitch not fucking your daddy!" my mother yelled, and I was like a raging bull as I charged at my fucked-up ass pops. These dirty bitches were going to die today!

Chapter Thirty

SIN

I was happy for my brother, my nigga did that shit! I can't believe he actually went through with it, to be honest. I thought he was going to change his mind, but he is a stand-up dude I have to give it to him. Because I be damned if I'm going to marry someone and my heart is with the woman I really wanted to be with. On my way out to my car, some chick walked up to me and asked me if I knew who Law was.

I asked her ass why; I'm not giving her no damn information on my brother. How the fuck she sounds, she just walking up on a nigga and shit. She mentioned Cassy's name, and I relaxed a little so I could find out what she wanted. She said that Cassy was her cousin, and she had a letter to give Law. She said Cassy came to her weeks before she died and gave her the envelope. Saying if anything ever happened to her make sure she delivered the letter to Law.

She walked off before I could ask her how she knew that Law was here. This whole Cassy shit was weird as fuck, I think I needed to look into this shit. I placed the letter on my seat and pulled off to go pick up Taymar. About ten minutes into my ride, my car was riding funny. Fuccckkkkkkkk! It felt like I had a flat tire, so I had to get off the expressway to check it out. When I pulled over and got out, my tire was damn near flat. I was mad as hell; it took me about twenty minutes to change it. I was finally finished and back in my car. Praying that I didn't get shit on this cream damn suit I had on.

I checked in with Cash, and he said that my money was safely stashed in the new warehouse. I breathed a sigh of relief after hearing that shit. All those years of grinding, I was able to make millions not only for me but for my brother as well. I dialed Tay up, to see if she was ready.

"Babe, I thought you said thirty minutes," she said when she picked up the phone.

"I'm sorry, baby. I had a flat tire, and I had to change it. I'm on my way to you now," I told her, and she was laughing.

"What's so funny?" I asked her.

"I'm laughing at Love's ass, I'm sitting here talking to her and my Grammy," she replied.

"Oh okay, tell them I said hello. Where is my nephew?" I asked her. After things settle down, I plan to pick him up and spend some time with him.

"He's in the room playing with his toys he got for his birthday," she stated.

"Oh damn, today is his birthday. I'm going to come in and see him when I get there. I will be there soon," I told her, I ended the call and turned my music up. I couldn't enjoy my damn music, because my damn phone kept going off.

"Yeah," I answered.

"What up?" my homie Trell asked.

"What up, nigga!" I stated, Trell was my muthafuckin' ace. It's been a minute since I have seen his ass. I was glad to hear from him.

"I'm down North at the bar, swing through. I need to put something in yo' ear," he stated.

"I will be there in five," I was close by and it would take no time to get to him. So, I decided to see what he needed to talk to me about. I pulled up in front of the bar, and text Trell to come outside. A few minutes later he walked out and hopped in the passenger seat.

"Bruh, what's the word?" I asked him.

"Yoo, you need to watch your back! Word on the street is this Tee bitch is coming after you and your folks! I also heard that Tee is not the connect, Jax is and she is a front for him. She's also somebody he's been fucking for years; I don't know how you got locked in with this shit but hit me up if you need me to help out!" he said, and I was still stuck on the fact that Tee was working for Jax all this time and they were fucking! Damn! I chopped it up with him for a few more minutes and left to finally pick up Tay. That information Trell just gave me fucked me up. I picked up the phone to call Law, but he wasn't picking up.

When I pulled on her block, all you could hear was shots being fired. AKs were letting off rounds left and right. I put my car in reverse and backed up as I got down low until the shots ceased. I hit the gas, as the SUV took off down the block. I wasn't sure who they were shooting at, but we were in the hood and these street niggas don't give a fuck about no one. I pulled in front of Ms. Josephine's house and got out. That's when I realized that it was her house that had gotten shot the fuck up! All I could hear was people screaming around me, and I took off running.

"Taymarrrrrrrrr!" I roared as the neighbors came out of their homes, and some were running to help!

To Be Continued

CONNECT WITH ME

Get connected with Author K. Renee
    To get VIP access of new releases, and sneak peeks please join my mailing list.
    Text KRENEE to 22828
    Website www.authorkrenee.com
    Facebook: https://www.facebook.com/karen.
renee.9421450
    Instagram: http://www.instagram.com/Authorkrenee